CATALOGUE
DIABOLIQUE

By
Marko Vignjević

First Montag Press E-Book and Paperback Original Edition July 2020

Copyright © 2020 by Marko Vignjević

As the writer and creator of this story, Marko Vignjević asserts the right to be identified as the author of this book.

Montag Press ISBN: 978-1-940233-78-9

Design © 2020 Amit Dey

Montag Press Team:

Project Editor — Charlie Franco

Managing Director — Charlie Franco

A Montag Press Book

www.montagpress.com

Montag Press

777 Morton Street, Unit B

San Francisco CA 94129 USA

Montag Press, the burning book with the hatchet cover, the skewed word mark and the portrayal of the long-suffering fireman mascot are trademarks of Montag Press.

Printed & Digitally Originated in the United States of America

10 9 8 7 6 5 4 3 2 1

1

⸻ ✑ ⸻

Focused inwards looking out, Mata Gradinar was putting the finishing touches on his Pedagogical Faculty graduate paper when – as prior engagements would have it – he was paid a visit by his friend Erroneous Petroneus.

But first a few observations on the working conditions of Mata, seeing how he was still but a student. He inhabited a small loft studio apartment for which his parents who lived in the countryside sent him money to sustain. Mata Gradinar never did like to discussing his parents, not even in front of his best friend whom he was expecting any minute. This did not stem from the fact that he felt as if he was somehow less of a man but rather that all who knew him – and knew he had no regular means of income – would make light of what he built up in his mind to be an undertaking of his lifetime, that thing being the graduate paper he was working on.

One thing that was true was his affinity towards children which had manifested itself when Mata was just still in high school. There was not a single moment during that period of his life that – upon seeing a young mother pushing a baby stroller

– Mata would allow a smile to ponder the future on his lips. As a young man he had learned to control this uncanny reaction for sake of being mistaken for someone who might have been touched in the head, as was said. It was also in high school that he developed an uncanny sense of when a particular teacher would go about conducting a lecture in a fashion that he, the great redeemer of enlightenment yet to come, would disagree with. That being thus, and without even knowing it Mata Gradinar was already subconsciously building himself into a pedagogue.

Nevertheless, and regardless of his – by now – burgeoning intellect, back home he was considered to be inherently stupid. His first ever job as a boy was to put commercial leaflets and flyers into peoples' mailboxes. And one would think this to be a simpleton's chore, but instead of putting fliers in all of the mailboxes once he would get into the building, Mata Gradinar would put leaflets only according to the number which designated the number of the building. In other words if the number was forty six he would enter and look for the mailbox with the same number on it, if he didn't find it he would leave the scene without even a blemish to his calm and collected cheeks.

Perhaps this, coupled with his chronic shyness around strangers, was the catalyst for his parents to send him to a big city for sake of Mata finding himself in one of the two most highly praised professions among all parents: those being either medicine or law. He, of course chose neither which his parents took as a compromise, propping up his pedagogical studies by the a fore mentioned monetary support, or as Erroneous Petroneus called it in jest, whenever Mata would go to visit his parents, his "dash for cash". In other words he, Mata, was always looked upon through the kaleidoscope of: Nothing can happen but everything cannot be.

2

⁓

His apartment was modest regardless of whether one was coming or going. There were mosquito nets on all the windows.

This day it was raining heavily which washed away the corpses of the unfortunate insects caught in the nets. But all that aside there was one much more important victim to the downpour in the appearance of one Erroneous Petroneus. Mata's friend wasn't even near the building of Mister Gradinar, and what is worse he had no umbrella or other means to shelter himself from the rain which was neither forecasted by the professionals nor was it expected by the general population. To make matters even more unfortunate, as concerned Mister Petroneus's visit, Mata Gradinar was taking a shower not so much for sake of hygiene – for he had already showered that morning – but for sake of massaging his first vertebrae strained from all the typing and rewriting at his laptop while working on his graduate paper. The unfortunate aspect of which being that Mister Gradinar couldn't hear Mister Petroneus's ringing on the intercom.

And so it was, much to his fortune, and lo to his rescue, came one of the neighbors who buzzed in Erroneous Petroneus of whom all in the building knew was a regular visitor and friend of one Mata Gradinar who himself was just toweling off when he heard through his worn out and decrepit front door the heavy footsteps of his friend.

Erroneous Petroneus was already done with his higher schooling and was well employed in the field of management. To put the matter closer to the reader's eye he worked in the Department of Risk Management at the Unionia Bank Plc. But rather than complain how easy it would be for him to take advantage of the system of risk assessment his bank used for his own purposes, Mister Petroneus held back firstly because he wasn't a risk taker by any means and secondly because he was well acquainted with the laws which governed the banking sector as a whole. Still, because it was in his nature, he would always joke and make light of how simple it would be for him to "steal the bank" as he would jest, doing so only in the private company of Mata Gradinar and only with regard to the Unionia Bank.

Rarely, if ever, would Mister Petroneus discuss his sentiments about the financial institution for which he worked outside the company of Mister Gradinar and, on occasion – if the occasion be a one of merriment and good humor – with Mata's girlfriend Alma Malarosa who took his comments at times to be the ones of a cynic and of a man who has something to hide. But irrespective of his better halves opinion, Mata Gradinar chalked it up – Miss Malarosa's stance on Mister Petroneus's views – to a woman's whimsy and folly for she was a student of the Academy of the Dramatic Arts also, and much like himself, in her final year of studies.

The shortest way to the longest distance is usually attained by means of self-delusion which wasn't the case with Mata Gradinar. Rising with the sun of Ilium he knew that the world was rising with him. He also knew, nay, he was certain that he heard the doorbell at his front door and only then remembered that he was in fact in expectancy of a friend. And so eventually it came to pass that Mata's hand would meet the key which met the lock setting and then there before his eyes an image of Erroneous soaked to the bone. It was here that the host rushed his guest post haste into his studio apartment.

"I thought we were a land locked country," Mister Petroneus protested. "What is this rainfall every evening business, I thought they had that only in the Scandinavias?"

"The trouble is not in the rain but in you not following the weather report."

"Who has the time to follow the damn weather report," said Erroneous defending his soaked position.

"Well, you for one. You never seem to get it right. I wonder why that is, seeing how you have more than opulent means vis a vis the old Roman adage "time is money"."

"True, true. But no one talks about the other side of that coin."

"Which is?" Mata Gradinar queried.

"Time is money indeed, but once you have money you find yourself lacking in time."

"I hate it when you know you're right. Here have a clean towel and dry yourself off, I'll just be a moment in the bathroom to get rid of this bathrobe and into my clothes."

As many of life's banalities dictate, Erroneous Petroneus was also not spared from the company of acquaintances – an obligation he managed to avoid that evening – but in general he didn't fall back on that option for sake of and want of advancement which at times made him feel like the first tree in the last forest on Earth. Brought up as a decent young man in a world too uncouth for him to bear, and it being how he was but an individual in it, Mister Petroneus knew he was going to have to conform to it. There was at one point of Erroneous's drying himself, a spot of an evil gleam appeared in his eyes as he stood in front of the mirror. Which he tried so desperately to rid himself of it for sake of not upsetting his host, but he knew that that particular expression of loathing in his eyes was or at least up until then held in reserve for his solitary ponderings about Unionia Bank Plc.

Once dry as it was humanly possible for him to be, Mata got out of the bathroom fully dressed and eager to hear of the goings on within the labor force of which he held high hopes to become a part of. With his evil gleam gone as an amber of a long-ago died fire, the two friends sat down for a cold brew, Erroneous Petroneus having a lot of questions regarding the paper his friend was presently finishing. For one, he wondered how come the work – which dealt with everything from the oldest universities such as the one in Padua to the ones giving electronic degrees – how come such an elaborate and yet concise graduate paper didn't, as yet, have a title.

"Did you know that Tolstoy wrote Ana Karenina without a title?" Mata answered with a question.

"If you're Tolstoy than it don't rain in Calcutta," Erroneous Petroneus replied.

"I see that a lot of time has elapsed since you attended a lecture."

"Yes, and I'm a better man for it."

"In what sense?" Mata asked.

"You wouldn't believe what goes on at work. And it's not just the mundane but also the illegal that makes one running for the foxhole of cynicism. Having said that let's not talk about my interesting job but rather I wish to know when are you taking your manuscript to the binders."

"As soon as tomorrow."

"I've seen a small binder's workshop on my way here. Do you know to which shop I'm referring?"

"Yes I do. It's the shop of the good old Bleh Fahmor; his family has been running that business since way back. And yes, before you ask, my parents have already sent me the necessary money to take care of that task."

After a lengthy conversation which included, for the most part, the questions and follow up questions on the graduate paper on the side of one Erroneous Petroneus; Mata Gradinar's best friend came up with a number of alternative titles for his friend's work one of which stuck in Mata's mind long after they parted for the evening. The title read: *Levels of Learning.*

3

⸙

Imagination is half of an idea. For sake of that notion Mata Gradinar turned on his laptop the next morning and typed the chosen words on the title page of his graduate paper which read: *Levels of Learning*.

He then got out his USB stick and transferred the document into its memory bank. Mata smiled at the thought of a "memory bank" in light of his prior conversation with Erroneous Petroneus, wondering what would happen to the world at large if his friend were put in charge of such a bank. As soon as he took out the USB the smile turned into a grin as he grabbed hold of his apartment keys and caught a glimpse of himself in the mirror. Mata headed pace, pace, to the nearby, neighborhood copy shop. He had decided to submit his manuscript as soon as possible to Bleh Fahmor the master binder for he knew that the old man would be in his shop early in the morning and had the habit of leaving his bookbinders' in the charge of his young apprentice well before lunch time.

The pavement showed no marks of the downpour from the night before, nor did the passersby, as Mister Gradinar made his way to the copyists' which was not far from the shop of Mister Fahmor's bookbinders (est. 1923).

Whilst in the midst of his busyness Mata's Cell phone rang, doing so repeatedly as he had some trouble getting it out of his pants pocket because, as it turns out, he had put on a few pounds during the course of time he spent writing his dissertation. When he finally managed to answer the phone he soon realized that he had plans for that night for it was Alma Malarosa on the other line reminding him that he promised to take her to the Cabaret Rose on the outskirts of town. He had completely forgotten about their reservations and thanked her for doing the thinking for the both of them, otherwise the relationship – in which she was the more understanding one – would have surely gone sour for the night. As Mata Gradinar walked into the printers their conversation was coming to an end. He received a bit of criticism because Miss Malarosa realized she had caught him off guard, in other words, caught him when he wasn't thinking of her – the actress to be.

It took some waiting but he stood on line holding the USB stick at the ready as if to say, "You people don't know what my memory bank here has in store." He did alternate his contraposto stance a number of times. Most of the customers were students, he surmised as much by their loudness as by their murmuring. When he was done they packed his paper, his work into a plastic bag and handed him the bill which he then paid; he immediately thought of his mother and father.

Once outside of the printers, he slowly made his way to Fahmor's Bookbinders. Slowly because upon consulting his wrist watch Mata realized he had plenty of time; a fact backed up by all the shops he had business with that day were right there in his neighborhood.

Coming up on 9:30 and Mata Gradinar was at the entrance of Mr. Fahmor's shop. He could see the aged gentleman hard at work through the glass portion of the front door to his shop. Mr. Gradinar entered with the entire charming chime which a proper bell hanging above the door provided. One look at the skull of concentration on Bleh Fahmor's face gave away all the financial misgivings Mata had regarding the putting the binding of his work in the charge of so seasoned a master bookbinder. But to the contrary, as soon as he heard the chime of his doorbell Mr. Fahmor stopped his laboring in the back room, handing it over to his apprentice, and rushed towards the front counter to greet a new customer.

Mata Gradinar put the printed material on the counter and explained what he wanted done to it. For his part, the aged master bookbinder took out a small booklet and pen from his shirt breast pocket and wrote down the price adding the date when Mata's book would be ready.

Mr. Gradinar was to come back in five days, the fifth day being Saturday.

4

T̄he night couldn't come soon enough for the two lovers, namely Mata Gradinar and Alma Malarosa. As was agreed they were to meet at the stop of the No.44 bus located right across the way from the building of parliament. Naturally Ms. Malarosa was fashionably late leaving Mr. Gradinar standing alone at the bus stop dressed in the one suit and tie he owned, the one his father gave him for his high school graduation. Suddenly, and after pondering the symbolism of the parliament building and its sculptures proportionately askew, there she was, running towards him in a beautiful sequin dress. Actually it wasn't made from one of those glimmering and shining sequin fabrics but actually was more reminiscent of fish scales both in structure and the intensity of glow. Alma Malarosa also carried an appropriate purse which she was clutching in her hand less she wanted to lose her footing while trying to maintain her balance on her high heeled shoes.

She embraced him and they exchanged a passionate kiss hello with Mata keeping an eye out for every and any bus which would pass by all the while.

"You look beautiful," he said to her.

"I swear I'll buy you a new suit as soon as I get into some money," she replied half smiling.

"Really. Have you had any offers for an acting gig?"

"I'm on the short list for a toothpaste commercial, or at least that's what they have told me."

"Good news?" Mata noticed a whisper of dismay in her words.

"You know how it is: "Don't call us we'll call you.""

"Here's our bus."

"Finally. I hate missing the openings at Cabaret Rose. They're the only ones in town who know what they're doing."

"How would you know?" Mr. Gradinar asked as they boarded the No.44 bus.

"From my days in Paris. Don't worry; we have loads of time to learn about and from each other. Sit, sit, sit."

And Mata sat down on what was one of the few empty seats on the bus with Alma hastily but not aggressively sitting down on his lap.

As was mentioned, the show was on the outskirts of town and with each passing bus stop the public transportation vehicle revealed more and more vacant seats so the two lovers didn't feel like barbarians in not relinquishing their comfort of sitting down to those among the elderly. They thought they could get away with everything that night. Counting on the laziness of another will get you nowhere. And knowing that it took her a crowbar to get Mata Gradinar to open up on any subject or aspect of his life which interested her, Alma Malarosa was the first to ask him about the progression of things regarding his graduate paper. She was pleasantly surprised to learn that Erroneous Petroneus had come up with the idea for the title of the work:

"Sometimes he has his moments," Alma concluded.

"He's a good man. You just have to give him a chance," Mata said.

"Give a chance to a banker, I think not!"

"But you do think regardless?"

"Regardless of what?"

"Of his position at Unionia Bank."

"That's all hogwash to my ears. Quick, I think ours is the next stop," she said.

Sure enough a monotonous prerecorded voice was disseminated through the speakers along the bus and the two lovers got up with Mata standing as if pasted to Alma's behind who was standing right in front of the exit. The bus door opened with a hissing sound. As soon as they disembarked Alma Malarosa began shimmering in her beautiful dress and Mata Gradinar took of his jacket to cover her bare back, now no longer a shiver.

They had to walk to the Cabaret roughly fifty yards from their bus stop but it was all worth it once they arrived. Cabaret Rose was full to the vault and the two lovers were shown to their table. Alma Malarosa returned Mata's jacket for such was the dress code, plus their brisk walk to the sight of the night's scene warmed her up nicely. Mata Gradinar gestured to the waiter and the couple was provided with finely printed and bound menus. Mata immediately thought of Bleh Fahmor the master bookbinder and how sometimes those craftsmen can be a little eccentric. But his mind was put to rest once Alma ordered drinks for them. Again this made Mata realize that she was the only person he knew who never made light of his financial status.

There were no announcements, no forward to be given or at least to explain to the patrons what was about to happen on stage; there was just a figure of a man dressed in a tuxedo with one side of his face painted black and the other painted red with a polka dot line running in-between. Much as every night, upon him setting foot onto the stage, a microphone descended hanging from a cable above his head and landed precisely at the level of his Adams apple made ornate by a bow tie. Having politely introduced the program for that evening the man was joined on stage by two young ladies dressed up in tunics with white powdered faces and bright red spots on their cheeks. They moved around him as if they were dolls, they walked from the hip and motioned their arms from the shoulders. The man at the microphone stood still as if he were a tin, toy soldier. One of the young ladies reached inside his tuxedo breast pocket and took out a cigarette case, while the other got out a lighter from the side pocket of the said piece of clothing. The man accepted what he was offered from. what they had found on his person and the two young ladies marched a stiff march off the stage.

"This is it, this is it," Alma Malarosa couldn't hold back.

"Oh, don't stir so much people will think we're newcomers," Mata Gradinar warned. Accompanied by a pianino the harlequin looking man who held out a cigarette between his thumb and index finger and his lighter also in his other extended hand began to muse of something in the following verse:

I hold poison in my hand
And I can smoke it if I choose
Now and then
But much to my dismay
There always comes a day
When the now and then
Become how and when

So I address this quandary to you
So that you might know it well
Whenever searching for things to do
One can turn to the stick from hell.

The audience went wild, especially seeing how most of them were already smoking their cigarettes. They began cheering him on, the man on the stage that is, with calls of: "Light up! Light up!" which he eventually did do, blowing circles of smoke straight into the microphone hanging from on high to the level of his Adams apple. The beautiful smoke plumes hugged and caressed the mic only to disperse once they rose to the wire which held it. It was then that the man announced his temporary departure from the stage, announcing next the Cabaret Rose "Honey Bees" as the dancing girls of that particular establishment were known.

The microphone was raised from the stage so as not to hinder the follow-up performance of the Bees who bore no resemblance to the famous insect but for one distinction: their eye shadow was made from golden leafs applied ever so attentively, and their mascara was jet black also applied in a way as not to ruin the gold leafs of the eye shadow.

As Mata Gradinar had promised Alma Malarosa the night didn't disappoint. They clapped, laughed and drank until the show was over. Hand in hand they walked back those fifty odd yards to the No.44 bus stop and upon boarding the bus once it came they sat down and shared the bench seat built for two pondering on their future life together.

When it was a matter of their future none of the two knew what to think, of course all they were sure of was that they wanted to stay together but they would always find themselves on thin ice when they would try to think of ways they could pull it off without the help of Mata's parents who – had they known he had a girlfriend – would immediately push for a marriage to be arranged and everything that follows, of course in his home town and under their family roof.

Neither Mr. Gradinar nor Ms. Malarosa wanted that to happen, which is why Alma didn't have any qualms about Mata not telling his parents about her yet. But it was one of those strange "yets" the kind that keeps dragging on until one of the parties in a relationship simply gives up through losing their patience. But where there was patience to be found there was also plenty of working grounds to go over before all was said and done.

5

⸺ ∞ ⸺

Pursuant of things close to his heart, Erroneous Petroneus had already set his sights on a beautiful blond girl who worked in a bakery right next to the Farmers Market where he would do all his grocery shopping. He dared not approach her. She looked so angry while she was in fact only too busy with all the other customers, whereas on the other hand Erroneous only thought of her in the context of them as a couple. But he wasn't so thick that he couldn't grasp the concept of a young woman working in a fast pace environment, and yet there was that part of him, the part of a little boy who wanted all of her attention.

Mr. Petroneus never spied on her, he never followed her after work; he just wasn't the stalking type. Besides, at one instance he did learn what her name was when at one point while standing in line on the sidewalk – for the bakery was a hole in the wall kind of shops – he heard one of her coworkers yell out her name and the name was Gabriela. Erroneous couldn't get enough of it, hearing her name ring out over the hustle and bustle of a myriad of customers, but he dared not address her by that name, he thought it would be too presumptuous on his part. And he was right for what he didn't know was that he had caught her eye as well it was simply a case of a well proven fact that a woman guards her emotions much better than a man.

Enough time had elapsed since Erroneous Petroneus learned her name that he knew he had to act on his *most* basest of urges, otherwise he realized that him holding back would either make him explode like a volcano or implode, causing irreparable damage to his psychological state which thus far held intact and he didn't want even the slightest opportunity to blame her for any changes in his state simply on account of him being a coward.

And then he was faced with a problem: should he approach her at her job early in the morning, such as should he show up first at the bakery on the off chance of catching her fresh and in a good mood, unsoiled by the crowds to come; or should he go about it in his old fashion thinking that she had noticed him as well and wouldn't mind the intrusion during her peak working hours.

It was Thursday night when – right before Erroneous went to bed – he decided to be the first in line at the bakery. By the by, he wasn't even sure whether they worked in shifts, that's how much the whole situation unnerved him.

Instead Friday morning he slept in. Not even recalling later on how he did it, Mr. Petroneus got himself together as fast as he could, shaved and showered with wallet in hand and was out the door straight to the bakery.

Gabriela was there. And much to his dismay so were the other customers, neatly standing in a straight line one behind the other as if to pay their respect to this goddess of the wheat staple everyone was taking for granted. And it was then and there with no pretense of forethought that Erroneous Petroneus decided to ask for her full name in the hopes of what will be will be. He was a nervous wreck as the line of customers grew ever shorter in front of him but he summoned up the courage and asked for one baguette:

"One baguette, please, Missus?..." he was being coy.

"It's Miss, sir, Miss Gabriela Tishma," she replied whilst tending to his order.

"Please don't look at me like that; I know I'm an ape. I was just wondering, when is your lunch break, Gabriela?"

"One o'clock. Why?" she answered and asked.

Erroneous knew he had to be tactful.

"I thought I could meet you here on your lunch break. There's a wonderful café nearby. Are you interested?"

"Yes, it's a date. Now go away you're creating a pile up in the line."

Mr. Petroneus was so beside himself with joy that he only then realized how long the line of people had formed behind him while he was talking to Ms. Tishma. It was only fortuitous that both their lunch breaks coincided otherwise he would've had to ask for the rest of the day off at Unionia Bank.

Upon returning home he put the baguette on the kitchen counter and tore a piece of it off for breakfast. It wasn't that he was hungry but he was starved for Gabriela's company. It's all in the wait anyway. Needless say but worth the mention Erroneous Petroneus immediately phoned Mata Gradinar to give him the good news, and seeing how it was Friday the two friends made plans for tomorrow to go and pick up Mata's *Levels of Learning* at Master Fahmor's Bookbinders.

But all future plans aside, Mr. Erroneous couldn't concentrate on any aspect of his Risk Assessment Manager's job at the bank. All he could think of was his golden blond, golden as a freshly baked loaf of bread, Gabriela. His situation wasn't aided by the fact that he knew that the rest of it was yet to come. Sure he made the first move and took the initiative, but how would he fare on their first date was the matter he knew nothing about. Erroneous Petroneus was overthinking both his future outlook and present prospects, meaning the future outlook regarding Ms. Tishma and the present prospects regarding his current performance at the bank.

All in all it turned out that his worries weren't unfounded which was brought to his attention when he was called into his superiors office for a tete-a-tete regarding a few but noteworthy slip-ups he had made.

"I realize that, sir. But the errors are corrected; I assure you," Mr. Petroneus said.

"Still, you look not quite yourself today, Erroneous, and you know how important Fridays are in our line of work."

"It won't happen again, sir."

"Go have lunch – a long lunch break just to clear your head. I'll have someone else take over your workload for today."

"Thank you, sir."

"Don't mention it and don't let it happen again," which was all Erroneous's superior had to say.

The café spoken of before where Mr. Petroneus and Ms. Tishma agreed to meet for the first time had a vacant table in the garden, right on the sidewalk of the boulevard. Erroneous saw her making her way, in no hurry, but not before he first spotted the free table. He gestured to her and sooner rather than later they were sitting one across the other under an umbrella shielding them from the midday sun. The beams of sunlight were penetrating in a display of the color green. Erroneous couldn't get enough of her looks, especially now that she wasn't wearing her work clothes which – as she explained – were not to be worn outside the bakery. She had her golden blond hair, let loose in cascades of waves down to her shoulders, now that she didn't have to wear her white cap from that morning while he looked quite her equal in his best suit. Both had just finished giving their orders to the waiter when Gabriela looked down at her wrist watch.

"Well, don't let me keep you," Erroneous said in jest.

"No, it's nothing like that. It's just that I have a stringent boss," she answered.

"I thought as much, so why don't we look at this get-together as a happenstance and not as our first date. And believe me my superior is the same way."

"Aren't you full of ideas. And your boss is as strict as mine, is he?" Gabriela Tishma asked.

"Who? Deda Blam? Trust me; he chewed me up just now before I came to meet you."

"They're all on edge because of these attempts to repeal the labor law, don't you agree?"

"Yes, I agree in all," Erroneous said.

"They want to change the trial period for new employees from three months to six. That really gets my goat!"

Erroneous Petroneus was astonished at her being in the know of current affairs to such a degree that he let the conversation move in the similar direction. Oh, and the waiter brought them their drinks.

"I know," Erroneous spoke, "they're pushing for reform which would give the companies more leeway in firing people. Can you imagine what strains that would put on the welfare system?"

"Well, as I say: We voted for it and now we've got it."

And with that concluding remark on behalf of Gabriela Tishma they slowly moved on to various other topics. It bothered neither that, at least at first glance, they didn't have much in common except politics, but somehow both found such differences to arouse immediate attraction towards the other. She came away from their first encounter with a sense of meeting a man who wasn't afraid to speak his mind even at the risk of coming off stupid. Ms. Tishma saw something in him which she couldn't explain but she knew she wanted more of it, and of course she also found out that he was employed, a fact which bore no concern on her either way.

Gabriela got up from the table and Erroneous was left sitting there gazing upon her leaving, but he was at one with himself because – naturally – they had exchanged phone numbers. He remained seated for a while longer wondering at her beauty and the somehow tomboyish, and yet at the same time, lady-like movements her body would make. He realized it immediately and murmured it into his chin below the power of voice:

"Oh yea, she's a traffic stopper and a jaw dropper."

6

While waiting for Saturday to come, Mata Gradinar spent his time going over his *Levels of Learning* on his laptop. He knew that what was done was done and being that the work was well in the hands of the bookbinder, he left well enough alone.

He spent Friday evening with Erroneous Petroneus in deep discussion over Mr. Petroneus's new acquaintance who was – as Mr. Gradinar concluded that evening – fast becoming his friend's first priority, namely Ms. Gabriela Tishma. Yes, Mata was eager to hear as much as possible about the new young lady in Erroneous's life, but never in his wildest dreams did he think he would get such an earful from his friend's physical description of her to what she thought on any and all of the subjects the two of them had discussed that day in the café near the Farmers Market.

"Well, did you kiss her?" Mata went straight to the throat.

"No, if you must know. Not yet."

"Then you're not a couple."

"Oh I get it. I didn't seal the deal. But I tell you, it wasn't easy, especially since I suggested that our outing should not be considered a date."

"Why did you do that? You know that you might be painting yourself into a corner, right?" Mata cautioned.

"I know and I intend to rectify that. We're going to a movie this weekend," Erroneous said not without pride in his voice.

"Oh, really? And what movie are you going to see?"

"You don't believe me, do you?! You think I'm making all this up: the beautiful girl, the stimulating conversation, the plans we made…"

"No, I'm really interested. Alma and I haven't been to the movies in…, I don't even remember how long. All they produce now days is idiocy," Mata said.

"A-ha, but there lies your problem, my friend. You and Alma have been a couple since I've known you, whereas I've yet to get to know my darling Gabriela better, so I'm taking her to see Hitchcock's The Ring. Let her make of the title what she wants, I've always been a great admirer of free association when it comes to human thought," Erroneous Petroneus stated.

All that and more was said between the two friends. But now it was Saturday's dawn, and with Alma Malarosa fast asleep in his bed, Mata Gradinar decided to fry her up a couple of eggs and serve them on the coffee table along with two pieces of toast with a curl of butter in between and a cup of black, sweet instant coffee, just how she liked it. In going through all Erroneous's tales of Gabriela, it seemed to Mata that they were but a pipe dream and wishful thinking of a young boy who just met someone whom he thought was his eternal lady love. It wasn't as if Mata didn't appreciate what had happened to Erroneous – granted he was a bit jealous – rather it was the complete lack of understanding of what it takes for a relationship to work on Erroneous's side which had Mr. Gradinar's goat. So without further ado, Mata Gradinar quietly left his loft studio apartment, desperately trying to keep the floorboards quiet, for the place looked as if it was falling apart, and it was indeed on its last shingles. On his way down the stairs he checked his wallet for the piece of paper which Bleh Fahmor had given to him on which were designated the date and, more importantly, the price of his services.

Once outside and leaving Ms. Malarosa to sleep in, Mata Gradinar found the street to be crammed with all variety of delivery trucks, the crews of which were in the midst of unloading fresh produce and groceries in all to the nearby supermarket. He wouldn't have minded it otherwise if it wasn't for those same trucks setting off car alarms on both side of the street which was just now becoming clogged in a traffic jam. But today it was as if nothing could faze Mr. Gradinar, so eager was he to see his *Levels of Learning* bound in hard cover of the color royal blue with the title and his name printed in golden type.

He wanted to savor every moment. Mata knew he wasn't on his own in his graduate project for his mentor had approved his paper long before he even learned of Fahmor's Bookbinders whose store he was surely approaching. Having gotten there he found the place to be a beehive of activity. It was obvious that Mr. Fahmor, who was usually in charge, wasn't there and he found a couple of students with disheveled student booklets who wanted them bound and made as good as new, but the apprentice refused to take on such a job for he didn't want to tamper with a legally prescribed document regardless of its condition. The same students were in a great state of shock upon learning of this new twist in what was obviously their long stay at university, for what else could bring about such wear and tear on an otherwise well-made student booklet so they left the book-binders, their heads bowed, and not knowing what to do.

Mata Gradinar didn't take this to be a good sign. Firstly, he wondered where Mr. Bleh Fahmor was because he was told, or at least he had surmised, that the master ran the shop in the morning shift. Secondly, the apprentice didn't instill a great deal of confidence in Mata, not if one takes into account the way he handled the students from just a while ago. Nevertheless, and with all nervousness put aside, Mata approached the counter thanking his lucky stars that there was no one behind him. He gave the aforementioned note written by the master bookbinder himself, along with the denominated price, to the apprentice.

"Ah, yes. Wait here, please," The apprentice said and disap-peared into the back room from which he shouted above the power of voice:

"Levels of Learning, right?!"

"Yes!" Mata shouted back.

"Here we go: Levels of Learning."

And just as Mr. Gradinar was to head out the door and say goodbye to the elongated shaped face of the apprentice, he decided to open up the extraordinarily well and tightly bound book which bore his title and name – it was blank.

There was no sign of a single letter, let alone a full text, to be found in between the covers of the thing. Mata Gradinar was in a state of shock, so much so that he lingered for quite some time, when suddenly, before he could even complain to the apprentice about his lost work there came in an onrush of young men and women customers leaving Mata Gradinar utterly defenseless and stupefied to the point of him simply exiting through the front door of the bookbinders' not believing his own eyes.

Outside he remained standing; going over the book page by page in much greater detail and in a desperate attempt to find something even resembling written material, but there was nothing, nothing except a straight line under which a footnote would normally stand, but in the case of Mata's book instead of the footnote there was written the following cursed thing:

Write your proposition here.

The only difference Mata Gradinar noticed (besides the missing text) was the paper of the book. The paper was much finer than he had requested and had an almost translucent quality to it. His order had been definitely reworked by the master but to what purpose he couldn't understand. And it was in that state, both of mind which manifested in his manner of walking, that Mata made his way home in the hopes of finding Ms. Malarosa in his apartment for they'd exchanged keys long ago.

He was in deep need of conversation with her. After all, she was the one who studied the dramatic arts and he was hoping – as he made his way, turning blank page after blank page, not even looking where he was going – that she might be able to shed some light on this issue of his. Hoping for a quick solution, he didn't mind the car alarms which were still going off around the place where those grocery trucks were still parked. Mata was unfazed by the honking of car horns behind the line of parked vehicles and the men laboring about the business of unloading more goods at as fast a pace as possible. Much to his delight when he returned home Mr. Gradinar found Ms. Malarosa at the breakfast which he had prepared for her earlier and was greeted by an egg yolk kiss on the cheek. She of course wanted to see the book, and upon receiving the feedback that there was nothing to see she said:

"Give it here. Let me have a look."

With much want in his heart Mr. Gradinar handed her the book, and much like him while he was at the bookbinders she was well impressed by the covers of the thing. But as soon as she opened the first page Ms. Malarosa, much like Mr. Gradinar came upon a stumbling block upon reading the instructions in the foot note on the first page.

"I don't understand. This could mean anything," she said to him sipping her coffee.

"I disagree. It is my belief that I need to find the correct proposition and see what happens next."

"Yes, my love, but that's not the point. You have a graduate paper to submit."

"I'll talk to my mentor with that regarding. I could always have that thing bound at the copiers, right?"

"Right," she answered.

"Did you notice something else about this book?" Mata asked.

"Oh I know, the paper is so fine. It's as if it wasn't meant to be written in, you know, as if no one is supposed to write anything down in it."

"I agree. And yet this proposition business is haunting me."

"I know. I mean the book covers are of your own choosing, correct?"

"Yes," Mr. Gradinar replied.

"Funny business that."

"How do you mean?"

"I mean that when and if ever you discover this supposed proposition the book will surely reveal itself to you."

"I don't understand," Mata was godfounded with every word she spoke.

"Ah, don't mind me. You know how we actors are."

Once she had finished with her breakfast, Ms. Malarosa washed and dried her hands and held the book in her arms, and it was in those arms that the book became heavier. She promised him she would ask her professors at the Academy of the Dramatic Arts whether there was any precedent, even in ancient mythology which could explain Mata Gradinar's predicament. She left the book with him upon her departure. They walked out together, she with her purse and he with his USB stick to make another copy and bind it at the copiers this time. This time it was serious because he needed to submit the finished work to his mentor on Monday.

7

⌒

Well on his way to the Pedagogical Faculty and with a backpack containing both the original binding of the *Levels of Learning* and its new copy from the printers', Mata Gradinar was heading to turn in his graduate paper and discuss the matter further with his mentor, Mr. Neven Goryan. A mild professor by nature Mr. Goryan would always indulge his students, whether it concerned the postponement of an exam they had to take or – as was the case with Mr. Gradinar – the handing in of an unbound graduate paper. In other words Professor Neven Goryan never stood high on formalities; all he was interested in was that the task be completed within a normal scope of time. Mata couldn't wait for the professor's reaction to the book he received from Fahmor's Bookbinders, coupled by his thoughts on the finished paper for which he knew there wouldn't be many – at least not in the shape of major comments – seeing how the two of them had already gone through it lengthwise and crosswise.

Having arrived at the building of the Faculty, Mata Gradinar was surrounded by his former colleagues or as he secretly called them in front of his friends: the perpetual students. There wasn't a soul within the circle which was becoming ever tighter around him that didn't want to have a peek at the graduate paper of the one who was to graduate at the top of their class. This was augmented even further; this stirring and excitement of his former colleagues by the fact that everyone knew he had originally written the paper without a title.

"Let's have a look at it, Mata."

"Give us a sneak preview, will you."

"No, just the name of the title will do it for me."

Those were just some of the comments Mr. Gradinar had to face until finally he was saved by the bell and all the former company had to disperse due to the signal that a new lecture was about to begin.

Mata didn't know whether Professor Goryan was even present at the Faculty that day. He was one of those academic types for whom the globe held no boundaries. For all Mata knew the professor could've been on a seminar somewhere, in which case Mr. Gradinar didn't feel quite safe about simply leaving his manuscript on Neven Goryan's desk in his office. In the hopes of finding his beloved professor – whom he hadn't seen outside the building – Mr. Gradinar entered the building of the Pedagogical Faculty and headed straight to Professor Goryan's office. He made his way through the empty halls behind the doors one could hear lectures or a brief comment by some student. Mata Gradinar climbed the stairs leading to his professor's floor and found the cleaning lady going about her business, as she always use to do in the four years during which he was a student there.

Mr. Gradinar stopped to say hello, "Good day, mam."

"Mam is busy, young man, so make it quick," the cleaning lady replied.

"You wouldn't happen to know if professor Goryan is in his office would you?"

"Yes he is. I just brought him his morning coffee. Wait, I know you."

"Excuse me?" Mata was taken aback.

"You're the, how do you say: Best in show?"

"Something like that, yes," the student smiled.

"I just don't know why you young people keep insisting on acquiring a higher education when you should be out getting married and having babies."

And it was then that Mata realized that he had talked himself into a corner. He thought long and hard before speaking or answering what he perceived was an offhand observation by the cleaning woman to whom the rest of the students wouldn't have given the time of day.

"So, do you suppose that the good professor has finished with his coffee?" Mata changed the subject of their little confab.

"Finished! Ha! He was done with it before I even left his chambers. That man waits for nothing and no one, so you better hurry."

"Thanks.".

All the cleaning ladies called the professors' offices 'chambers'. It wasn't something which was mandatory, quite to the contrary, the only ones worthy of inhabiting a place the upkeep of which was in their charge were precisely the professors and hence the uncanny custom of the cleaning ladies and cleaning ladies alone calling their offices 'chambers'. No one dared to even attempt to change that practice. It was an unspoken agreement between all the parties concerned, the parties being both the students and the professors.

Having said that, Mata Gradinar went on his way in the hopes of catching Professor Goryan in his office and was pleasantly surprised — upon knocking at his door — to see the aged man still finishing his coffee and gesturing for Mata Gradinar to come in. Sitting at his desk and surrounded by books placed and neatly organized on all the sides one can imagine a room to have, there was Professor Goryan gesturing to Mata Gradinar to take a seat opposite him at the desk. Mr. Gradinar didn't need further instructions, it being how the professor was still finishing his coffee, so he unzipped his backpack and took out all the contents thereof laying them out on the table.

"Much too soon, much too soon, Mata. If you don't mind, I'm just finishing this mug of coffee and then we shall proceed with your business," Neven Goryan said.

"Agreed. You don't mind me having a look at your library, Professor?" Mata asked. To which the telephone on the professor's desk rang and he gave Mata a nod in the affirmative before picking up the receiver.

Mr. Gradinar couldn't believe the titles which were represented on the shelves. There were books on every possible subject from text books on children's education to titles on family planning. No small wonder that Mr. Gradinar and Professor Goryan had such good rapport, which was made even more so enhanced by the professor picking up the copied version of Mata's graduate paper and reading its title. Needless to say but worth the mention that upon casting a gaze on the title, the professor hung up the receiver and severed the line of communication with whomever was on the other side of so short a stick.

"I see that you came up with a title," the professor stated the obvious.

"Yes. I just hope it's not too bold for a graduate paper."

"I accept such a point of view. It does sound more like a PhD title than anything else."

"Yes, but do you accept it in light of the text and its subject matter? I mean we've been poring over it for quite some time," Mata Gradinar asked.

"Consider your paper accepted. Now you'll be defending it on the sixteenth of this month. How does that date suite you?"

"It suites me fine, professor."

"Now, what's this version here? Is this the one that came from the bookbinders?"

"Yes, but it's the strangest thing, when I picked it up and had a look, there was no text to be found except this foot note right here on page one which, as is my estimation, I'm suppose to fill out myself."

The professor took a closer look and uttered the words written down, below the power of voice, "Write your proposition here?"

"What do you make of it, professor?" Mata asked.

-"'m afraid that, as is, I don't understand what it means," he conceded. "And this is how they gave it to you at the bookbinders?"

"Yes, it is."

"The most astounding thing with regard to this document is the high quality of its paper," Mr. Neven Goryan said.

"Do you have any advice for me on this subject?"

"I'm afraid not. I deal in other subjects, not in speculation or anything even resembling things pertaining to fantasy. All you need to remember is to show up here, in my office on the sixteenth."

"Same time as now?"

"Yes. And don't bang your head against the wall concerning this hard cover version. The panel will gladly accept any version of text as long as it's bound together in some shape or form. You did well by making another copy."

"Thank you, that is all I needed to hear. Until the sixteenth then, Professor."

"Precisely, same time, same place. And don't be thrown by the large auditorium. Many a student wants to hear what you have to say."

"Of course. Goodbye, Professor."

"Goodbye, Mister Gradinar."

Mata packed the hard-bound copy of a book as yet empty and headed out of Professor Neven Goryan's office. On his way down he met the cleaning lady again, but was in a hurry to meet with Erroneous Petroneus in which he hoped to find out more about his friend's new romantic interest, and his first proper date with Gabriela Tishma.

The cleaning lady was in the middle of washing the floor and was doing so behind a warning sign which read something to the effect of "slippery" or "wet, mind your step" and as he was passing by her he heard her comment as if she was talking to herself:

"Books, books, all these people care is books. Am I right, young man?"

"Yes. Especially about the books that are as yet to be written."

"Oh, do be on your way!"

"Yes, mam."

It was at that moment that the bell rang again designating the end of a portion of lectures for that day. Mata Gradinar knew he had to make a run for it if he wanted to avoid the inevitable questions of his former colleagues all of which – and this he was sure of – would probably be pertaining to his conversation with Professor Goryan, a much respected and revered authority at the Pedagogical Faculty, predominantly among all the students.

Mr. Gradinar slipped just once at the entrance of the building, but didn't fall, all with the backpack containing the strange bookbinders' version of his *Levels of Learning*.

That very same night, the evening of the day Mata Gradinar handed over his work to his Professor; he made plans with Erroneous Petroneus to meet at Club 88 for drinks and what he hoped might be Petroneus's clarification on the matter of the bookbinders' version of his graduate paper which he decided to take along with him. But beforehand, before he set foot outside, Mr. Gradinar took out the note pad he used as an aid in writing the damn thing desperately trying to find some possible clue or even a solution as to what to write in that foot note. As he combed and pored over every single note, Mata Gradinar didn't even realize how fast time was going by when he heard his cell phone going off. It was Erroneous, already waiting for him at the club at their table. To this Mata had no other choice but to make his apologies and invite his friend to come over to his studio apartment. After giving Mr. Petroneus the leeway to complain and comment on the down sides of his studio apartment, Mr. Gradinar promised his friend that the drinks would be waiting for him in any shape or form. The fact that the shape and form of the spirits Mr. Petroneus had previously asked for

were expensive didn't factor in to Mr. Gradinar's equation for —
regardless of him living a seemingly independent life — he was
still a man kept by his parents, and generally well supplied in that
department.

After making his apologies and explaining the reasons as to
why he thought it best that they should meet at his place, such
being the mystery of the foot note in his *Levels of Learning*, Mata
Gradinar listened to his friend talk for a while about Gabriela
Tishma. Suffices to say, and this was a fact Mata wasn't proud
of, he let his friend talk on and on about his new romantic relationship simply because he wanted to exhaust the topic once
Erroneous Petroneus arrived and they talk face to face. As brief
as their phone conversation was from which Mata deduced that
Erroneous had already had a few to drink, so was Mata's venture
to the liquor store down the street. Not being able to discern
what his friend was in the mood for precisely at this time, Mr.
Gradinar bought a nice bottle of apricot brandy instead. Thinking that would be enough he turned away from the shelves
where the hard liquor was on display and had a look at a long
line of customers being tended to by a very new and inexperi-
ence cashier.

He didn't want to be the one to complain, which was most
hypocritical of him, being how he always voiced off in such
situation, rather in seeing others in front of him voicing their
disappointment in the young girl minding the till Mata Gradinar found it to be a perfect opportunity to keep quiet. Mr.
Gradinar's only worry was that Mr. Petroneus would arrive
before he was finished with the purchase. And then suddenly,
as if by a miracle, the young cashier was due for her break
and was replaced by an older, experienced woman. So was it
that the line began moving faster than a cheetah through the

African savanna. Now it was the unprepared customers, perhaps lulled into a state of sluggishness due to the tempo up until then who were to blame. They scrambled for their bags placing them neatly on the counter, and they couldn't find exact change in their wallets that were buried down deep, etc. Seeing all this develop, Mata Gradinar decided to make ready like a paratrooper about to be dropped behind enemy lines. Having remembered the price of his apricot brandy – which wasn't hard to do seeing as it was the only article he was buying – when it was his turn, he was on the line handing the aged woman the bottle and the exact amount of change.

"This is all you kids need, more alcohol!" she commented reprimanding.

"All with good measure, mam, I assure you," Mata replied.

He didn't see it, but as he was exiting the store his comment made the old cashier smile well after he left, as if admitting the fallacy of her prior statement. Besides, they were neighbors, she worked on the street he lived on and all the above-mentioned was only a part of their rapport.

As much as his unblemished eyesight permitted, while returning to his building, Mata Gradinar could've sworn he saw Erroneous Petroneus heading his way. But it wasn't so. What he in fact saw was a local wino weaving his way around the pavement clutching at parked cars one moment and then holding on to the walls of buildings the next. All the while he kept repeating:

"The key is the function of the lock. The key is the function of the lock."

The drunken man could not have been avoided and he headed straight for Mata. Not wanting to be rude, or on the other hand, not wanting to bump into the staggering fellow, Mr. Gradinar decided to walk the few steps remaining to his building

by moving counter wise of the movements and the rout the wino
had chosen for his path. But in the end they did pass each other:

"The brandy, the brandy. Have they raised its price?" the
man asked.

"No. The price is still the same and so is the outcome," Mata
remarked.

"You damn people and your puritan preaching. Out of my
way!" and the wino pushed Mata aside as if this one was a goose-
down pillow.

Bumped as if hit by bull, Mata Gradinar hit the wall of his
building, though he managed to salvage the bottle of brandy he
carried in his bag by clutching it near to his chest. He did damn
near dislocate his shoulders upon his being slammed into the
wall. While climbing the stairs to his studio apartment he found
that he couldn't forget the wino's words and the truth with
which they now resounded in his ears: "The key is the function
of the lock."

Perhaps that was the solution he was looking for; the magic
words to be written in the ever ominous foot note of his bound
but blank book. Besides, Mata knew that he would probably
never see Mr. Bleh Fahmor, the bookbinder, again and why
should he, keeping in mind that his graduate paper was already
handed in and was ready to be defended on the sixteenth of that
month.

Having panted to the top floor – for Mata Gradinar was in
very poor physical shape – he saw Erroneous Petroneus standing in front of his front door with his thumb, ever so often,
pressing the doorbell.

"You can stop with the ringing I'm right here," Mata said.

"Pardon me, but one never knows where you'll be or turn up
next," Erroneous reciprocated.

"Here, hold my backpack while I get the keys," Mata said and smiled as he mentioned the word "keys".

"What did you buy for us to drink?"

"Apricot brandy. I'm sure it'll be to your liking," Mata said as he handed him the bag containing the bottle.

As they entered the damp, humid studio apartment their conversation went on as if nothing had changed regarding their surroundings even though Erroneous Petroneus hated his friend's humble abode.

"Tell me about Gabriela Tishma, and don't forget anything," Mata said thinking his suggestion would make for a fine ice-breaker, and he was right.

For the next hour Mr. Gradinar had his ear bent by Mr. Petroneus and his latest conquest – although to be clear, a conquest of a non-carnal nature. Erroneous talked of how they went to see Hitchcock's *The Trouble With Harry*. He also mentioned that he walked her to her door which was where they kissed. Apparently Ms. Tishma shared an apartment with a couple of roommates which – as Erroneous made an effort to clarify – didn't bother him in the slightest seeing how all the roommates were females.

Mr. Petroneus then suggested that Mata and Alma join them in what was apparently a Hitchcock tribute festival, or so he explained. Having heard his friend already making future plans for all concerned, Mr. Gradinar began pouring the brandy liberally. But before any more brain cells were lost he grabbed a piece of paper and a pen in order to write down the words of the wino he had bumped into in the street. When he was finished he showed the phrase to Erroneous.

""The key is the function of the lock'. What does that mean?" Mr. Petroneus asked.

"I thought I'd write that sentence in the foot note of my *Levels of Learning* hard copy. What do you think?"

"Truthfully I think that this whole business of your graduate paper stinks to high heaven and back. Did you consider going to speak with Mister Fahmor on the matter?" Erroneous asked.

"No. I have not."

"And why not?"

"Because there's something strange about his workshop."

"How so?" Mr. Petroneus asked.

"First you bring in your work to have it bound…, nothing special just your typical brand of paper, and then suddenly you get this kind of quality from a master bookbinder.

"Here, feel this quality and then tell me if this is something you've ever come across." Mata got out his book from the back-pack and handed it to Erroneous for a kind of inspection, after all Erroneous had played a huge part in the making of the book itself or at least that's what Mata felt with regard to the title of the work. And once he held it in his hands, the aforementioned quality didn't skip Erroneous's notice. In fact, Mr. Gradinar felt a kind of eerie respect delineating itself on his friend's face.

"What's wrong? You look like you've been seen by a ghost," Mata asked.

"I'm not sure, but I think that you shouldn't mess around with this thing, whatever it might be. Look at it, doesn't it seem to you to be slightly aged, because it doesn't look like a freshly bound book to me."

"Give me that!" Mata said as he tore the book out of Erroneous's hands.

Mr. Gradinar opened the first page and without as so much as a shiver in his hand took the pen and finally wrote in the foot note the phrase "The key is the function of the lock." Mata waited for a while and filled up both their glasses with apricot brandy once more; he was looking for courage after the fact, after the deed was done. And then he put the book down on the coffee table as it was in his lap a minute ago waiting for something to happen when, all of a sudden and miraculously words began appearing on the inner portion of the title cover of the thing, words which read: Have it answered. Not knowing what that meant the two friends looked on as page after page began displaying a grid pattern each containing a number of columns with specific instructions as to what needed to be written inside each of them.

9

~~~

What being as it was, Mata asked Erroneous to leave him alone with the book, which this one did taking with him the bottle of apricot brandy. Having seen his friend off, Mr. Gradinar found that he was in the worse place possible, alone with his thoughts and the cursed book just waiting to be filled, lying open on the coffee table. He didn't know what purpose the book was meant to serve, and just as bad, he didn't know whether he'd get to see Mr. Fahmor the bookbinder again for at least some kind of instruction regarding the matter. In other words, it all seemed like a big coincidence to Mata. First his best friend comes up with the title, then the mix up (or at least what he thought was a mishap) at the bookbinders and all of that coupled with a kind of palliative responsibility he was now feeling for he didn't know how many people were actually aware of what was now in his sole possession.

Considering all that Mata Gradinar decided not to write anything down in the book. For now he wanted to remain in a state of utter speculation – again, because he didn't know the purpose of the thing. There was however one option he did take into serious consideration and that included letting his dear Alma Malarosa in on his secret. But then again he wondered whether to expose her to the book, being how he loved her so much as to obligate her with such potential knowledge as — what was written on the inside cover — "Have it Answered," and what that might entail.

Mata Gradinar picked up the book and went through all the pages, each was still empty of words, though each now had on it a printed grid with the exact same headings for every one of them. The book itself did look a bit aged to which Mata opened it again and shoved his nose right in between the pages. Erroneous had been correct, his *Levels of Learning* did indeed have a smell about it reminiscent of an old edition which had spent a better part of a lifetime on the smoker's shelve.

When he had had enough of banging his head against that particular wall Mata locked the book inside the studio's credenza. He then decided to call Alma Malarosa, which he did, and arranged for a Norwegian salmon dinner at his place. It was the first time Ms. Malarosa learned of Mr. Gradinar's culinary savvy which, as she had put it to him exchanging kisses over the phone, was as yet to be proven.

After hanging up the receiver Mata found out that he was capable of keeping the secret and wondered whether the same could be said about Erroneous Petroneus who was also with the knowledge about the book. Knowing that Erroneous was still not at home Mata phoned his cell and got a slivering, drunken man's reply. They spoke thus:

"Erroneous, can you hear me?" Mata asked after his friend picked up the call.

"A-ha, it's you. My best friend who has cast me out of his home," was the reply.

"No, that's not what I'm calling about…"

"Well, what do you have to say to me?"

"I'm sorry, I truly am. It'll never happen again," Mata promised.

"Too late now, I'm not returning your brandy, never and for nothing in the world. Ha, ha!"

"Listen to me, Erroneous; this has nothing to do with us having drinks a while ago."

"That's so typical of you. First you give an apology and then you take it back. Well not this time for I and I alone intend to finish this bottle. And furthermore it is you who doesn't understand. You have no idea how hard it is to work in a bank, especially as a Risk Assessment Manager…"

"Stop and listen. I've decided to follow your advice and to not to use the book for now."

"What book? Oh, your precious *Levels of Learning*. Well, have it your way, chum."

"Okay, just promise me you won't talk to anyone about it. Especially to Gabriela Tishma," Mata said half-pleading to an obviously tipsy person.

"Ah, my Tish. I think I'll give her a call. You have my word. Now off with you, sir, I'm in the middle of unlocking the front door of my building and I tell you it's no small feat."

"Thank you, Erroneous, you're a good friend."

"Knowing you, Mata, that statement might turn out to be true."

"I'll talk to you later."

"Later is always too late. Call me tomorrow," Mr. Petroneus demanded.

"I can't, I have plans with Alma tomorrow."

"There, you see: Later is always too late. That's why they call it later."

"Goodbye, Erroneous."

" Good Bye."

The last thing Mata heard over the phone was the opening of Petroneus's front door before he hung up. Afterwards Mr. Gradinar remained standing in an about-face position directed at the credenza, the key of which was clutched in his hand. It was as if he was speculating on what was going on inside, what was going on inside that book of his. To cool down and to tend to his everyday hygienic needs he decided to take a shower before going to bed. Mata didn't question such a decision on his part even though he had showered that morning. Only upon exiting from the bathroom, all wet and in his bathrobe did he have a good look at his apartment and the state in which it was. First thing tomorrow he was going to clean it, all some-odd square feet of it. It was as if, as soon as the book came to life, he has let himself go. Mata left the key to the credenza in the bathroom medicine cabinet and gave it no further thought, no matter the irony of it, which wasn't lost on him.

He sat down and turned on the TV, but nothing could take his mind off the book, not even the evening news. In fact it was the news which spurred his imagination as to what he should write down in the book next. Obviously it was going to have to be something regarding the Ministry of Education. Such were the directions his mind was taking and therefore Mata Gradinar picked up a small pad and pen and began developing and writing down the list of things which he was going to put down in his *Levels of Learning*. But the news on television kept coming at him so fast that he was barely able to take his notes, let alone discern between those of significance and those of no importance. What did catch his ears – for he was looking at his small pad while listening to the news – was the inordinate number of scandals and affairs at the highest level of government.

Hearing of all these, Mata brimmed with confidence at his emerging thoughts. He wrote down a note which read "The Merchant Court" of which he knew from before was the most corrupt Court in the land. It seemed to him, as he went from thought to thought, that he was already filling his book, which to his knowledge remained safely in the darkness of the locked credenza. It also appeared to him that no one knew about what he was able to do with his book for he had already paid for it so he figured it was now his sole property and not in the domain of any other individual or institution.

For the first time in his life while lying in his bed fast asleep, Mata Gradinar was slowly learning what it is and what it feels like to have power and have no one else but one know about it. When he slept, he dreamed of the Norwegian salmon he was going to prepare for his Alma Malarosa and the next day he woke up with an erection.

10

⁓

On his way to the Farmers Market, and having made sure of his shopping list now tucked away in his back pocket, the first thing Mata Gradinar saw in the street was a couple of homeless people rummaging through the dumpsters. Mata realized that what they were looking for was food and nothing less, but least he wanted his Norwegian trout dinner with Alma Malarosa to fail, Mr. Gradinar passed them by without an offer of assistance when suddenly he heard a child's voice yelling out from the dumpster:

"The key is the function of the lock!"

"What's that?" his old man asked.

"A piece of paper," the child replied from within.

"Leave it, it's only garbage."

As he heard that sentence read aloud by the child Mata realized that someone besides him and Erroneous knew about the book. And how could they not if a vagrant family could come across it in a no less than a written form, the same form in which Mata Gradinar had written it only a while ago. Still, not wanting to get involved with the family of homeless people, he just passed them by. But he couldn't help but feel fear and a butting suspicion that something was about to go terribly wrong. And so as he progressed on his way to the Farmers Market he remembered the wino from whom he first heard the now infamous phrase and the fear he was feeling was even more amplified when he remembered that the wino had had no breath of alcohol on his breath, none whatsoever. But that didn't have to mean anything. Still, all beside himself with dread, Mata Gradinar rushed back to the dumpsters and offered the father a hundred dinars for that particular scrap of paper.

"What does a gentleman such as you want with that type of garbage?" the father asked with the boy still in the dumpster.

"It's just something I threw away by mistake last night and now I need it."

"Hey, man, it's your money. Son, give that piece of paper to this here gentleman."

"Here you are, sir," said the child as he reached out and handed him the piece of paper.

"And here's your hundred, as promised. Please excuse the interruption, but I must be on my way," Mata Gradinar said all the while turning around.

"Best of luck, sir!" the child yelled after Mata.

"Shut up and get out of there. We have our daily bread now. But you did good, son."

As Mata was making his way to the Farmers Market he was holding the mildew ridden, wet from all the other garbage and sticky beyond all comparison, piece of paper not knowing where to put it. He paused at the pedestrian crossing on the Thrashing Floor right before the Market and – for reasons unknown to him – he turned the wad of paper around only to find, much to his chagrin the words "Have it answered" written on the other side.

"Christ on a cross!" resounded from Mata's mouth.

And it being how the shout was heard by all who occupied the Thrashing Floor at the time, Mr. Gradinar quickly shoved the paper in his pants side-pocket and almost landed in front of a car for such was his shame regarding him bringing so much attention to himself.

The breaks of the oncoming car screeched and the car horn was more than audible to all waiting to cross the street where there was no traffic light. Of course, Mata Gradinar was the last to join the rest of the pedestrian traffic, and with a quick bounce in his step, and a tout bag in one hand and a raised palm gesturing his apologies to the driver of the other hand, he too managed to cross the street unscathed but still deeply concerned. Truth be told, once on the other side he needed a moment or two to recompose himself, the stench of the wad of paper in his side pocket radiating throughout his surroundings. Luckily the Farmers Market was there where he now found himself and he headed straight through it for he knew that the smell he carried with him would be lost, or in the least merged and amalgamated with the already preexisting smells of various produce on offer in the Market.

The Market itself was jam packed with customers. Most of the people there were pensioners who had the time to spare and money to save, unlike the youths who mostly did their grocery shopping in the supermarkets. On that note it needs to be said that the aforementioned crowd of people was moving very slowly from booth to booth, while the farmers were all a roar, advertising their goods. This is mentioned only in the context of the need for one to know their way around the Farmers Market, less they'd rather spend a whole morning amidst the green booths.

Mata Gradinar was making his way south-bound to whence the smell of fish was coming from. And, indeed, he could portend the large aquariums in the distance and a fishmonger waving his cleaver up in the air and shouting in the form of an argument with one complaining customer.

He slowly approached the stand, walking along the cobble stones of the Market and proceeded to pick and choose among the fish laid out on display in their ice filled crates beneath which a refrigeration system was blowing cold air for regulations sake.

"What do you need?" the fishmonger asked Mata.

"Is this Norwegian salmon?" Mata pointed at one of the fish in a crate.

"Indeed. Yes it is. Now what do you need. Be quick about it, I've got a line of customers waiting."

"I'll have two hundred grams of your Norwegian salmon, please."

The fishmonger smelled worse than the products he was selling. It was only fortunate for Mata Gradinar that no other customer turned and looked at him funny due to the smell of the now famous wad of paper that he had purchased earlier. And all the while – the while he spent waiting for his order to be taken care of – Mr. Gradinar was wondering what to do with that piece of paper once he returned home. Should he destroy it somehow, perhaps put it to flames or dispose of it in some other fashion, he didn't know because he feared what such an act would do to his book for he didn't know how his bound, hard copy version of *Levels of Learning* came to be the way it was anyway.

"Here you go. Two hundred grams of Norwegian salmon. Next!!!" the fishmonger shouted.

Mata paid for his fish and decided to look for other, recipe related ingredients, on his way back home while browsing and looking around for the cheapest deal because he had already given a hundred dinars to the homeless father and son tandem and paid even more dearly for the Norwegian salmon. However he knew he wasn't leaving the Market, not just yet. Eventually he bought all the ingredients necessary for his recipe when – on his way out of the Market – he heard girl-chatter coming from the back side of the bakery. Normally Mata Gradinar wouldn't have made anything of it; he knew that the girls were likely on break, but he paused when someone in their company yelled out, "Tish!"

This immediately reminded Mata of the nickname Erroneous had chosen for his new girlfriend which made him want to see her. With this in mind he positioned himself behind a nearby booth containing mostly watermelons and from there he could easily spy on the group of girls, especially on the one he had identified as Gabriela Tishma for he saw her turn upon hearing her named yelled out. It was one of the other girls asking whether she, Tish, had a cigarette to spare.

Seeing her like this, Mata Gradinar saw without a doubt what had attracted his friend to this young woman. Now he felt the responsibility to see her on her own unencumbered by the company of any male companion so that he may refer back to Erroneous what he has learned. There was only one small flaw in his plan: the farmer behind whose booth he was so obviously hiding didn't appreciate anyone loitering about his place of work. Having had enough of Mata's pretending to look at the watermelons the man began raising his voice in order to chase Mr. Gradinar away from his booth. It being how the watermelon booth was near the back entrance of the bakery, some of the girls began to turn their heads as if to inquire on whether there'll break out a fight or something of that nature. But Gabriela Tishma drew

back their attention with tales of her evening out with Erroneous Petroneus much to the pleasure of her listeners.

It was in this way that Mata Gradinar fled the scene once he
made sure he wasn't spotted by any of the girls for he too purchased his bred at their bakery. And hence he made his swift exit
from the Farmers Market in a state and overall excitable condition much similar to the one in which he came in.

11

.... ⟨⟩ ....

Meanwhile, Alma Malarosa treated herself to a day of shopping for new lingerie to wear to her evening with Mr. Gradinar. She decided not to go alone into her venture but rather she went with her best friend Neli Nizdlak. Walking the streets, they both decided to treat themselves to a cappuccino at Grinet café. Being good friends with Alma, Neli hadn't wanted to turn down such an invitation, especially if it meant getting out of the house and having some of her time spent away from her husband of two years, Oli Uzdlak. They had barely began their tour of the shops when the discussion was getting ever deeper, all of which, well not all but most of which, concerned sex and the usual and at times adventurous practices thereof by the two couples. Alma Malarosa was eager to hear how does one keep the flames of passion alive in marriage while Neli Nizdlak wanted to know a little bit more about Mata's fascination with Scandinavian and Northern women in general.

"I love the things my husband does to me," Neli whispered to Alma in one of the stores.

"Then how come you didn't take his last name?"

"Because I like going against the grain."

"You know what; I see nothing here that I like. Let's move on to the next store," Alma said.

"Oh, sweetie, you should be looking for a boutique not just some store."

"Fine, if you say so. I'll blow my budget anyway. You've always been a chore to go shopping with, and yet, your choices were always right."

"You are buying lingerie for this night only, right?" Neli asked.

"Well, yea, but I hope it'll last me for more than that."

"Not with your Mata's fascination with those Scandinavian women."

"You're right. Why do I always take him to those Sava Shumanović exhibits at the National Museum I'll never now. That's where he was first bitten by the bug of the perpetual blond type with fair skin and…, oh, never mind!" Alma was getting frustrated.

"My sentiments exactly. What's wrong with us Singinas, the Belgrade women?"

"Nothing a smooth Italian couldn't fix," Ms. Malarosa said.

They both burst out laughing and bended at the waists in hysterics when they came upon the front entrance of La Perla, the mother of all such boutiques, as concerned those two when it came to a premium choice of undergarment for ladies. Entering the store they felt as if they were two princesses only this time the toy castle was real and they real in it. Everything had an aroma to it. Every corner of the boutique seemed to radiate a certain scent which was provided to the clientele as if to enhance firstly their shopping experience and secondly to increase the number of items purchased. Once inside they found that they needed to speak below the power of voice. Even outside of the boutique there was nothing and no one except for the drivers waiting on other ladies still inside, sitting prepared for their return at the wheels of some of the most luxurious and exquisite automobiles. But nevertheless, all the frippery aside, Neli Nizdlak wanted to hear more about her girlfriend's and Mata's sex life. Alma Malarosa was more than reserved to discuss the issue in the store for she had always thought that her voice was too deep, even when she would whisper. On the other hand – as she explained to Mrs. Nizdlak – there was nothing worthy of mention as concerned her and Mr. Gradinar's bedroom activities.

"Why would you keep such things from me? I've shared with you, haven't I?" Neli whispered in a far-off corner of the store.

"Oh, sure. But it's different for you and Oli; you've been married for two years."

"What do you know about married life? And why are we whispering. You know, just because all of us are in a store of a foreign brand name doesn't mean that we're still not Singinas."

"Fine," Alma relented, "what do you want to know?"

"How big is he?"

"Let's just say that he has changed me forever."

"No?!"

"Yes. He's ruined me for other men," Alma said blushing.

There was an awkward silence between them in which Alma Malarosa picked out an outfit of fine white cotton and a lace pair of bra and panties for purchase. That is how they exited the La Perla boutique.

"C'mon, Grinet is not that far away, let's sit down and have a drink, Singina," Alma suggested.

"I guess…, let's."

"What is it? You didn't expect to find that out about my Mata, did you? Well, next time choose your questions with more care."

"Let me just make a call," Neli got out her cell phone.

She placed a call to her husband Oli Uzdlak. They probably had one of those nonsensical conversations daily which are usually provoked by nothing. Now she was talking baby talk into the phone and just above the power of voice in order to take some of the pressure off of her shoulders:

"What are you doing, Oli, my oxen?"

"Vacuuming the apartment, darling," her husband answered.

"Then I won't keep you, baby. Bye," Neli said.

"Bye.- the husband reciprocated.

"There, you see. Do you know what my husband is doing right as we speak?" Neli asked Alma after hanging up the phone.

"No."

"He's cleaning the apartment."

"Good for him. And though you haven't asked, I'm sure my Mata will walk down that same isle with and for me one day," Alma said.

"Again, what you're saying just now goes to prove that you know nothing about married life."

"Okay, I concede," Ms. Malarosa decided to put the topic to bed.

Once at their table at Grinet café, and having given their orders to the waiter, Alma Malarosa's Cell phone began ringing in her bag. She didn't hear the sound of her phone ringing at all until Mrs. Neli Nizdlak brought it to her attention. When she got out her phone and answered it her face was set alight and her lips expressed a smile which her best friend had never seen before on her for she wasn't the type to show emotions lightly and for no particular cause. The call she had received was in fact a call back from her audition for a tooth paste commercial. Alma Malarosa couldn't wait to surprise Mata Gradinar with the good news, and she would've called him immediately had Neli not interject and stopped her in her intent.

"But I want, nay, need to tell him that I got the part," Alma said.

"Leave it for your dinner tonight. That way you'll have more things to discuss."

"I don't think there'll be much discussion tonight between me and Mata."

"Again with this. Why don't you rub it in my face!" Neli Niz-dlak sighed as she spoke.

"Okay, I will do just that."

And Alma Malarosa leaned into her girlfriend's ear, covered her mouth with her hand and began whispering in ways of more than just simple innuendo, letting a line of discussion delineate on Mrs. Neli Nizdlak's face. It was as if Alma's girlfriend was saying – and doing so with no words uttered – that whatever they choose to do tonight is their business. She only cautioned her about safe sex. *Always come prepared*, and it being how Alma and Mata have been together for some time now, such things were understood, you know, regarding family planning and such.

"You know, it wasn't always a picnic," Alma started up again once their waiter had returned with their order.

"What's that?"

"You know…, his size."

"Really?"

"Of course not. It hurt like hell at first."

"You don't say?"

"Oh, yes. The only reason I stuck with it was because I loved my Mata Gradinar."

"You mean to say that most women don't enjoy it when it's so big?"

"I wouldn't think so, no. I mean, most normally developed women wouldn't."

"Thank you, sweetie. That's a load off my mind."

They sat, talked and had their drinks with the La Perla shopping bag as close as it could've been to Ms. Malarosa's freshly waxed calves. And what both of them took away from their meeting was that, unlike a male sex organ, which is a sponge; the female sex organ is of muscular tissue, so there.

12

⌒

He was impatient for her arrival, Mata Gradinar was, and it had nothing to do with his Norwegian salmon cooling off or the dinner getting spoiled. He was eager to see her because they were in love, and though it might sound pathetic and trite, Mata couldn't wait to hear yet another Shakespeare joke from his Alma Malarosa. The ringing of the intercom couldn't come soon enough so when it did he pounced, leaping through the air of his small apartment to buzz her in. He would always feel a bit ashamed whenever Alma would come by, ashamed by his apartment, his overall financial status, it being how he was still a kept man, kept by his parents regardless of the fact he didn't live with them anymore. But such was his predicament and with every echo of Ms. Malarosa's shoe heels through the stairwell Mr. Gradinar would cast such thoughts – thoughts uncouth for the company of his lady – aside and let the numerous tomorrows that were going to come worry and sort them out for themselves.

The doorbell rang and he answered it by opening the door. Suddenly, like a wolf in sheep's clothing ripping them apart right

in the middle of the flock, Alma Malarosa jumped Mata Gradinar. He didn't protest, as men rarely do on such occasions, but
he did manage to close and lock the door of his apartment. Her
legs were wrapped around his waist and she could feel his bulging, burgeoning member growing as if to rip apart the slim fit-
ting mini dress she had on.

Mata grabbed her by the hips and began rubbing her against
himself while all Alma Malarosa could do was sigh, take deep
breaths and whisper the words of love into his lips for they were
not kissing, no, it was always that way when she had something
to say. He navigated the apartment, the floor plan which he knew
by heart, with ease and confidence and took her to where they
landed, right on the couch where she remained astride of him.
Upon exchanging a barrage of kisses wherever they had bare
skin to kiss, he undid the back zipper of her tight dress out of
which she slipped with greatest of ease and where she proceeded
to put a condom on his penis by using her mouth.

She found that he was fully prepared for the evening, (he
was in the habit of shaving certain aspect of his privates), that
is fully shaved as she crouched above him and found her resting
place on the "impaler", as in "Vlad the" for that was what she
had called his sex organ. Truth be told her rest didn't last long
and pretty soon Alma was loveforging him like never before, and
she felt it not to mention anything more Mata who was so taken
aback by this sexual assault that it was all he could do to keep up
with her. Mr. Gradinar knew from before that Ms. Malarosa gets
this way after seeing a romantic movie, but he dare not speak a
word about it nor ask some stupid question.

He may have been a kept man but a fool he was not. After
a while he rolled her over and was on top of her sweaty and still
sweating body. The mosquitoes were trying to penetrate through

the nets on the windows but to no avail even though the smells which Mata and Alma's bodies were giving away were drawing them in like looters. At least the young lovers had an audience. Mata pushed as gentle as he could when she whispered in his ear:

"Faster."

To which he replied, "Harder?"

Ms. Malarosa blew up her cheeks knowing full well that if he were to go harder she would have pains later on when he spoke into her eyes.

"Let's leave the 'harder' to the animals, okay?"

She grabbed his rear first and then his face before letting out a roar as if it were high noon in the Okavango and the roar was one of, "Yes, oh, God, yes!"

They finished simultaneously with one small difference and that was that Mata ejaculated outside of Alma, as he backed away completely. Mr. Gradinar was always fearful of running into a faulty condom which is why his idea of safe sex was – besides the use of a condom – coitus interruptus.

She would always complain to Neli Uzdlak about how the two of them never came together, how Mata always pulled away from her which was affront to the high quality of sex they were enjoying, or such were her feelings on the matter. But as Neli said to her once, "Until you're not ready to talk to him about it the problem is entirely yours. So confront him already."

Mata Gradinar and Alma Malarosa got dressed. She decided not to bring to the fore the above mentioned dilemma she had about her better half. One by one they went to their bathroom to wash their hands, for dinner was already waiting on them to begin, which in a way they already have.

Mr. Gradinar didn't have a proper kitchen table; there was just a counter top where the now slightly cooled Norwegian salmon was waiting to be put to the test of every affinity Ms. Malarosa was aware of regarding the likes and dislikes of her lover. She was stupefied by how good his cooking was and in a humorous rapport he congratulated her in the likewise on her new upcoming toothpaste commercial and hence he insisted on her telling him a new Shakespeare joke.

"You're not going to like it. It's not that funny.," Alma said.

"Please, humor me," he insisted.

"By the way, what became of your graduate paper?"

"Oh, forget about it. But you will come to my defending of the thing won't you?"

"Yes, and thank you for inviting me. When will all this be taking place?"

"On the sixteenth of this month."

"And are you prepared?"

"As prepared as this Norwegian salmon. By the way, how is your dish?"

"Superb," Ms. Malarosa said.

"So, let's hear it, another Shakespeare joke, if you Will. Ha,ha, no pun intended," Mr. Gradinar said coming off as a bit slow.

"Okay: What did Shakespeare's father say to his wife?"

"What?"

"Help me, help me; there's a William in my Shakespeare!"

Mata Gradinar nearly choked on a mouthful of potatoes so Alma Malarosa poured him some more wine and began slapping him on his upper back.

"Marvelous. That's one of your best ones so far. Bravo!"

"I propose a toast."

They both raised their glasses as Alma continued, "To us and our good health, and to the rest at our behest."

"Hear, hear!" Mr. Gradinar shouted.

Their two glasses met in a chiming ring of the translucent matter and it was as if a promise was made right then and there, a promise which was suppose to keep them together forever as Ms. Malarosa thought, and a promise which was suppose to keep all other temptations away from them as Mr. Gradinar interpreted it.

13

⸻ ❧ ⸻

To stay the duration of keeping his *Levels of Learning* book a secret – along with that smelly wad of paper, the stench of it could still be sensed from the credenza – a secret he had shared only with Erroneous Petroneus, Mata Gradinar needed to arrange for a much soberer meeting with his friend in order to discuss what was to be done with the bound version of his graduate paper. All Mata knew was that the matter would be best dealt with after the sixteenth of that month, a date which came, at least according to Mr. Gradinar, like a comet streaking through the sky. On that day he got up before the cock, the red eye of the sun not even visible on the horizon. He then shaved like he had never shaven before, and to look at him was to think that he was but a young man attending high school. On that particular denomination of a numerical nature on the calendar Mata Gradinar specifically called on all of his friends which included both Neli Nizdlak and her better half Oli Uzdlak, requesting repeatedly for them not to come to his defense of the graduate paper.

Alma Malarosa was the only one he would allow into the auditorium on that solemn date. With all the forced exclusion of his peer group, someone could think that he was going to demonstrate how to split the atom and not talk about current models in education. But regardless, she decided to be there for him, just as he had promised to attend her graduation play at the Academy of the Dramatic Arts.

As far as Mata Gradinar's choice of dress was concerned, he had only one navy blue suit given to him by his father for his customary pram night way back when he was still living in his home town which made him think about his parents, well, at least about his old man and how he shouldn't fail them having come so far to rank at the very top of his class. It was a very simple, light suit, the tie having been provided by Erroneous Petroneus who was also on the black-list as far as attendees of the proceedings was concerned. Quite frankly Alma Malarosa was a bit angry at Mata Gradinar for not inviting everyone whom they knew because she wanted so desperately to show him off. Regardless of her wishes he remained stubborn as a mule, but still, to see him in that navy blue suit and Erroneous' tie made her wish to tell the people who were beginning to gather around the place where she was sitting in the auditorium that they were indeed a couple. But Alma Malarosa kept quiet in the back row of the floor seats, sitting patiently and looking at him, actually getting a better view at the scruff of his neck than anything else, only to enjoy the fines – or at least that's how she saw him – the fines of the contours of the side of his jaw and the perfection of his earlobe, a jaw, by the way, that didn't clench, not even at the sight of the professors coming into the auditorium and taking their places on the bench across and high up above Mata Gradinar.

My poor love, was what Alma Malarosa immediately thought, he was as if surrounded by these old people who, somehow in her head she figured, wanted ill of him, and wanted him to fail. At one point she wanted to boo while the Professors were taking their seats but held back thanks to a young lady who asked to pass by in front of her in order to be seated net to one of her colleagues.

One of the highlights of the defense of his paper was the example Mata Gradinar gave regarding Galen, the ancient Roman surgeon. Mata talked, doing so at length, at the end of the proceedings using Galen as an example of dogma in science. He stated that due to the genius of the ancient surgeon who, Mata didn't forget to mention, nearly discovered the human circulatory system, the very artisanship of science (which was how Mata categorized medicine) remained stagnant for three hundred years for that's how much time it took for the medical calling to get out of Galen's shadows. The audience of his fellow students was captivated by what Mata Gradinar was saying. Of course there were some questions on the part of the Professors but even they were reticent to interrupt such an eloquent and well thought out defense. Alma Malarosa even heard some of the students in the jam-packed auditorium whispering, "This should be a PhD thesis not a graduate paper." And it was due to her eavesdropping that she learned how highly Mata's colleagues thought of him and again how critical they were of him. The latter was proven to her when she heard a comment in this vein, "He always jumps the gun. This is too good for a graduate paper."

"That's why he's graduating at the top of his class and you're not," Alma Malarosa said below the power of her voice.

Nobody in the auditorium knew who she was nor did they care, but most couldn't agree that she was right. And all the

while, sitting alone in front of the Professors, Mata Gradinar
was discussing the first-ever universities, such as the ones in
Padua, Oxford and Cambridge, and the benefits of collective
learning. Among those present were not only students of the
Pedagogical Faculty of Belgrade University, quite to the contrary, in those seats was everyone who could get in and listen
to one of the most brilliant young minds in academic life of
Serbia at present. Needless to mention but worth the note, is
that there were also representatives and headhunters from various companies both domestic and foreign there at the ready
to make him offers. Now what would a company want with a
graduate of the Pedagogical Faculty was up to them to distin-
guish and devise. All that needs to be said about that sixteenth
was that Mata Gradinar was in the zone. He answered every
follow-up questions that the Professors had, and at times, as
others had noticed, he even jumped ahead of them knowing
exactly what they were going to ask.

"I must say, young man, that we're fully satisfied with your
work and the manner in which you've presented it here today,"
one of the Professors stated.

"Thank you, sir," Mata replied.

Alma Malarosa was so excited she could barely contain herself from jumping up from her seat and applauding. But then
another professor had a more potent question to ask, "Just
one more question if you will, Mister Gradinar, and then we'll
adjourn: How on Earth did you come up with such an elegant
title for your paper?"

Alma clenched her fists hoping that Mata would shrink away
from the truth, that he would limit the mention of his friend's
playing a hand in something which obviously left such a great
impression on the Professors.

"The title of the work came from my best friend," Mata said without a break in his voice.

"Oh? Really?" the Professor who asked the question reacted with surprise.

It was Neven Goryan who came to Mata's rescue by adjourning the comity of the Professors by saying, "Your friend did you a great favor. Congratulations, Mister Gradinar, you've passed your defense with a perfect ten."

Whereupon another Professor added, "And this work, these *Levels of Learning* shall be deposited in the Pedagogical Faculties library so that it can be viewed, read and admired by your younger colleagues for ages to come. Again, my personal congratulations, Mister Gradinar."

"This comity is now adjourned. Congratulations," Professor Goryan concluded.

And at the sound-out of those words by his Professor, Mata Gradinar stood up only to be greeted by the full auditorium standing up as well and giving the young man a salvo of applause, shouts and whistles. They were cheering the great one who was now being approached and congratulated by people he didn't know, attendees at other Faculties at Belgrade University who he had never seen before. It was utterly harmless, or so he thought until – and this he could've sworn was real – he saw Mr. Bleh Fahmor sitting in the back in an olive green rain coat and while others were applauding Mata could've sworn he saw the master bookbinder rubbing his palms together with purpose and intention.

As Mata Gradinar was trying to make his way towards Mr. Fahmor, the master bookbinder rose and left the auditorium and a face popped up right in front of his. It was the face of his Alma Malarosa. She was all aglow which was partly due to the humidity in the auditorium which didn't have any air conditioning. She took him by the hand as they went outside, again to the salvo of applause, until they were in the safe haven of the surrounding boulevards.

Alma Malarosa wanted, nay, insisted that she treat him to something sweet so they headed to the Pelivan pastry shop. It was her idea but it was going to be his treat, which he insisted, and she didn't protest for she knew how much this day meant to him. Alma was miffed by only one thing, and that was that she didn't have an appropriate Shakespeare joke to tell. At the bakery, they gorged themselves on sweet macaroons and Mata's favorite: the Turkish tulumba. Neither thought about leaving the table or proceeding for some kind of walk, no not in the slightest. Alma and Mata were just sitting there reveling in his success and her upcoming toothpaste commercial, feeling that their future had a lot of promise yet to be fulfilled.

14

···················· ∽ ····················

The sixteenth had long passed along with his defense of the graduate paper. By now Mata Gradinar was supposed to be working as a teacher, at least at a grammar school level but he had decided to postpone it in part due to the original edition of the *Levels of Learning,* the purpose of which he still didn't fully understand. However, every so often, and when he was alone he would take the key from the medicine cabinet and unlock the credenza below the TV set taking out the said book and going over the pages. And what was once just a wad he had purchased for a hundred dinars from a homeless family had already turned to dust, becoming so hardened and fragile that he could barely touch it.

So Mata Gradinar decided that he should burn the wad of paper in his toilet. At first he was fearful of the effects this act might have on the book as a whole so he took the full text along with him to the bathroom in order to look for any changes, if at all there were to be any which there hadn't been already. After igniting it, the wad fizzled away in the porcelain edges of the toilet and then floating on the bowl water turned into a charcoal black crumple after which Mata Gradinar flushed the toilet and the burnt offering down with it whereupon he decided to air out the entire apartment.

It was already mentioned that he was expected by others to be working already but – for reasons of letting himself go due to the fascinating confidence which he drew from the book – there was no talking to him. Everybody had tried to reason with him; from his own Alma Malarosa through Erroneous Petroneus and his now not so new girlfriend Gabriela Tishma to the only married couple among them Neli Nizdlak and especially Oli Uzdlak.

But all Mr. Gradinar wanted was to stay at home and love-forge with Ms. Malarosa; a secret he conveyed only to Mr. Petroneus who – while showing understanding for his fellow male and the needs thereof – tried to convey what was going on with Mata to Alma even if he did hate playing the part of the go-between regarding anyone especially the two of them seeing how one was his best friend. And how was he to be honest with the young Ms. Malarosa and not mention the book, which Mr. Gradinar still kept secret from the world in his credenza. Faced with such pressure, particularly the kind coming from his own Gabriela Tishma whose attitude was, "Why even get involved?" which showed to Erroneous how little she understood about his stance towards anyone he, Mr. Petroneus, considered a friend – much to his disappointment. That being thus, Erroneous Petroneus decided to make a surprise visit to his friend, Mr. Gradinar, despite the efforts of Ms. Tishma's trying to sabotage his plans by proposing that they should go out that evening instead.

"No, I haven't seen him for far too long. I must go and at least check up on him," Erroneous said.

"Have it your way. Is it alright if I invite some of my girl-friends from the bakery for an evening in?" Gabriela Tishma asked.

"Of course, Tish, we are living together, isn't that right?"

"Right it is. Kiss me before you go," she said.

That's the sendoff he had received at home, but Erroneous wasn't concerned with it much, what was weighing more heavily on his mind was the reception he would get at Mata Gradinar's place. Of late he had learned that Mata knows how to hide the dirt and filth of his otherwise unclean apartment. How he was able to hide all that needed to be cleaned Erroneous didn't know, all he was certain of was that every time he would visit the apartment it was spotless and with no trace of anyone's effort, or so it seemed. Another thing Erroneous had noticed in his visit to his friend was that Mata Gradinar didn't even bother to turn the bed into a couch anymore. As if to keep it a signal that any female who walks through his front door better be ready for Mata to pounce on her like a leopard. Thirdly and perhaps most impor-tantly, Erroneous was wandering – doing so in no small instance due to the phone call he had received from Mata that time he was drunk – about his friend's *Levels of Learning* and what, if anything, had or was to become of that book. He didn't feel at ease at all in asking and inquiring as to whether Mata Gradi-nar had begun asking and writing down question into the damn thing for which he saw less and less practical use with every passing day, except if one was to use it as a force for extortion somehow and as soon as that thought penetrated throughout his mind he found his index finger on the button in the behest of the name Gradinar. Mata buzzed him to come in and three brief but demanding flights later the two friends didn't fall short of a warm embrace in the shape of a bear hug.

"Thank you for staying away from my defense of the *Levels of Learning*, I sincerely appreciate it. Did you know that you were mentioned?"

"Me, at your Faculty? In what context was this?" Erroneous asked.

"One of the Professors wanted to know where did I come up with the title. So naturally I said that you, my best friend, named my work."

"So it hasn't still gone to your head I see, much to the contrary of what this bed here displays."

"Oh, relax. C'mon we'll sit at the counter in the kitchen. I've got beer," Mata said.

"So, what's next for you?"

"I haven't decided yet. I'm leaning towards returning to my hometown, but Professor Neven Goryan keeps telling me that there's a new PhD program coming up at our Pedagogical Faculty that I should consider."

"I've heard, Unionia Bank will partly cover the costs of all the stipends. But to the otherwise how's your overall health. You look as if you've put on a few, what's going on?"

"It is my belief that that is all due to the cursed bookbinder's version of my graduate paper. The more I postpone opening it and asking it questions – of which not even I'm sure what they are supposed to be – the heavier I'm getting," Mata explained.

"Tell me, have you had any offers of employment from the private sector? Anything at all?" Erroneous asked.

"No, why? Do you think I should be applying for positions outside of academia and academic life?"

"All I'm saying is that I think we could put that book of yours to better use if you did or were to decide to go job hunting in the private sector."

"Yes, that would be something. Imagine, finding out every skeleton in their closets and then have them interview you. Ha, ha, ha, the very idea sounds intriguing," Mata Gradinar said.

After both friends had taken more than their fair share of swigs of beer, Mata Gradinar excused himself in order to check his E-mail. And as he had suspected there was a new note, one from his parents, urging him to take the government job, preferably one with a PhD program stipend.

"Look, would you just look at this. How can I explain to my parents that I won't be able to repay everything I owe them through a government stipend, the funds of which would be allocated towards a PhD," Mata said.

"Well, by what they wrote back to you, it doesn't seem as if they're looking for their money back. I think they just want what's best for you."

"But you don't understand. Four years of study, the rent, the food. My god the food! Only in Serbia is the food cheaper at the Farmers Market than in the supermarkets."

"And this worries you why exactly?" Erroneous asked ironically.

"I don't know, old friend. Maybe I just care too much."

"You do realize that they're expecting your answer, do you?"

And with that small push and a shove, Mata Gradinar wrote back to his parents stating in the E-mail that he would be pursuing a further academic career, but that he would also be looking for work in the private sector – with noone knowing that what Mata termed the private sector he meant the *Levels of Learning* and his finally unleashing the power of that book.

The two friends hung around Mata's place for a while longer and parted right at the point at which Erroneous would have had too much to drink. Mata Gradinar cautioned his friend not to mention the book to anyone, not ever, for which he received a stark agreement from one Erroneous Petroneus. It was also agreed upon their parting for the day that Mr. Gradinar was not to begin using the *Levels of Learning* bound copy without the expressed knowledge of Mr. Petroneus. They made a pact to which both parties could easily adhere, the only difference being that the damn book was already taking its toll on Mr. Gradinar while not much has changed in the meanwhile about neither the appearance nor private life of Mr. Petroneus. And though Mata was well aware of that he nevertheless decided to stick to their agreement no matter how those dice may fall. Regardless and to no consequence to Mr. Petroneus they always seemed to fall in the favor of someone less, except Mr. Gradinar who knew, or at least thought, that if he were to pick up the book and pen he could change his outlook for the better with an ink-stroke of a pen. But as his character demanded he would do no such thing as yet, at least not until necessity drives him to it, which was something both friends were aware of, even though those and such words remained unspoken between the two of them.

15

⌘

ata Gradinar had to learn all over again how to will himself to take care of his apartment and his belongings. This wasn't on the account of the *Levels of Learning* which still remained hidden, nor was it because any of his friends, his girlfriend or Neven Goryan, his Professor. No, rather it was due to the fright he began to feel towards Mr. Bleh Fahmor, the master bookbinder whom he could've sworn he had seen once disguised as a wino and once applauding in the auditorium upon him, Mata, successfully defending his graduate paper. It was solely because of him that Mata Gradinar began taking his future career seriously and, by the way, had decided to burn that small wad of prophetic paper in the toilet. And he felt all this pressure on his young shoulders simply for lack of acknowledging when a transaction began, when it took place, and when it ended.

The stated above is a reference to the *Levels of Learning* and the transactions with it regarding. Mata Gradinar couldn't help but feel that he was indebted to the old master bookbinder, but on the other hand he knew not to seek him out again for he had tried that approach before and it hadn't worked. As before there would always be the ever-present apprentice at the shop who would wave Mata away saying, and more likely lying, that Mr. Fahmor wasn't there. But what proved Mata Gradinar's fear was that on one such occasion, while simply strolling through his neighborhood, he came across another bookbinder's store under the same name, this was in Kumanovska Street. Just for curiosities sake he peeped inside and sure enough he saw Bleh Fahmor teaching an even younger apprentice the secrets and the skills needed to become a bookbinder. At that point it was as if Mr. Fahmor truly didn't recognize Mr. Gradinar and so he shouted at him, "We're not open for business yet!" Mata didn't think much of that particular shout and he calmly replied just before closing the door uninterrupted, "I hope my *Levels of Learning* are serving you well. You do good work Mister Fahmor." And with that he simply closed the door.

After that one brief to and fro, Mr. Fahmor ran into the same street clutching at Mata's shirt sleeve trying to explain why he did what he had done to Mata's graduate paper. He talked of promises of greatness and of true, unsoiled power if he, Mata, didn't abuse the book. Mr. Fahmor went on to explain further that Mr. Gradinar's *Levels of Learning* was the finest piece of writing by a student, seeing how most students only skim their work with an eye towards passing, and that they don't reach deep down and truly build a foundation for something in the future with their writings and that's why he had wanted to 'build him', so to speak, a bound book of which even the greaet Gutenberg would be amazed.

"So, Mister Fahmor, which one of us is the pilot shark?" Mata Gradinar asked having stopped his walking away, the old man's hands still gripping to his sleeve.

"Please, sir, let's not turn this into rivalry. And please use the book for good."

"For good, he says?! I would rather you have me cleaning up after the elephants at the Zoo. That would be an easier task. For good? Ha."

"And why do you consider our book to be a task, sir?" Mr. Fahmor wanted to know.

"Firstly, it is my book and my book alone. I paid good money for it and will make whatever use of it I choose. The very audacity that you should even hint at this being some sort of project of ours is preposterous to me, Mister Fahmor."

"But you don't know the materials I used in making your book into what it is today. You know nothing of the fabrics or the stitching or the thread. Why, as I understand, Mister Gradinar, you weren't even the one who titled the book. So you see it is as much mine as it is yours, as it is the person who gave it a name."

"Be that as it may in your mind, of which I wish to know nothing more, but the book itself is in my possession. And seeing how I am not a selfish man I'll share the spoils of what I catalog in it with my best friend who, as you duly noted, named the book. But I do wish to see less of you, sir," Mata Gradinar said and with that his sleeve was released from Mr. Fahmor's tight grip.

As the two parted ways, Mr. Fahmor to get back into his new shop and Mr. Gradinar to head to lunch at Leskovachki Roshtilj, Mata's cell phone rang in the sound off of a text message which, as it turned out, was from Alma Malarosa. He stopped mid-sidewalk, not paying attention to the young mothers pushing their baby strollers from behind him, but in the end he did adhere to common courtesy and placed his person next to the gates of the

Nikola Tesla Museum from whence he read the message which was in lieu of his upcoming – well it was not exactly upcoming so much as it was tomorrow – birthday.

The text message wasn't so much a text as a list of guests Alma Malarosa wanted to see on his birthday party, and as Mata Gradinar knew from prior experiences, when she gets her mind set on something she usually gets her way. Reading further on, the party was going to meet on Resavska Street and board the No.3 streetcar which will take them to the Topchiderske No□ i restaurant where she had already made reservations. It was going to be a select group of people as she said in the message, so as not to freak him out. Among those present will be their regulars: Erroneous Petroneus and Gabriela Tishma, Neli Nizdlak and Oli Uzdlak and the two of them. And the message ended in typical Alma style which read, "If I don't see you until the streetcar stop wear something warm and dress in layers, they're forecasting an overcast evening."

Mata Gradinar pasted himself away from the gates of the museum as soon as he read the message and as soon as he saw a group of tourists beginning to line up in front of the building. By and by his stomach was growling and a large number of tourists, at least those who kept quiet and heard that growling and mistook it for Mata's passing wind, which couldn't have been further from the truth. He knew well enough not to apologize but instead moved swiftly across the pedestrian crossing of Prote Mateje and briskly, pace for pace, found himself on the other side. There there was an electric pole right opposite the crossing under which he was now passing. Its wires seemed to present a favorite haunt for the local pigeons. Those with much experience of walking the streets in that neighborhood knew to hasten their steps while walking under wires populated in great numbers by those rats of the sky. While, on the other hand, those among the pedestrians to whom this was an unknown neighbor-hood almost always ended up with the task of getting out their tissues and whipping the pigeons off-casts from their persons.

Once on Beogradska Street, Mata Gradinar turned a sharp right corner and headed straight pass the Medical Book book-store, and after making headway in the very moist afternoon, he finally reached his destination. Entering he headed straight to the counter and gave his order after spying an empty table. A young and attractive waitress served him his hamburger in toasted buns and was soon on her way to the next customer, to the next table.

Mata took out his cell phone, in case of any uncertain emer-gency, which was around the time he realized that he had forgot-ten to answer Alma Malarosa's message. He put his food down and texted her back saying in his message that he was at lunch and that later on he would be in a short meeting with Neven Goryan, his Professor, with regards to his new position at the Pedagogical Faculty. As soon as he sent the message he knew he had made a mistake. Mata immediately expected his phone to ring at any moment with Alma on the other line embolden-ing him to take the job offer, any job offer that they might have given him. But he was surprised as to how collected and calm she took the news, for all he received back for his text explana-tion was a little smiley face which looked like this:

$$(\; ; -\mathbf{x} \}$$

Which was Alma Malarosa's "say no more" symbol. And the texting between the two of them halted right there and then at that point for the time being.

16

The time of their meeting at the No.3 streetcar stop on Resavska Street was given to Mata Gradinar by his Alma, so despite having a bunch of other things – such as his run in with Mr. Bleh Fahmor – on his mind there was no room left for excuses, even though Alma knew that he might just try and get out of the party she had put together for him. Without any other option Mata Gradinar dressed; again wearing his old man's navy blue suit which he wore at his defense of the graduate paper. He wasn't superstitious or such and other but it was the only article of clothing in his possession which was appropriate for special occasions, so he wore it. He double checked the credenza before leaving the apartment, and just to be on the safe side, he took the key to it out of the medicine cabinet and shoved it inside his pants pocket. All the way down the stairwell he couldn't help but worry what if someone were try to break into his apartment. His suspicions didn't require any imagination, for instance: it could be Mr. Fahmor himself, or it could be one of his apprentices, or Mr. Fahmor and his apprentices working in tandem.

The noise of the street didn't calm his worries much, but, on the other hand, it did command him to leave his ill-thoughts behind and focus on the traffic, both pedestrian and especially motorized traffic (Belgraders are the worse drivers). But in his mind – now adopted to the new surroundings – Mata Gradinar was still thinking about the cursed *Levels of Learning*; something for which there was little time for he had already accepted the job offer from his Professor Neven Goryan to serve as his office aide until he gets his PhD in pedagogical science and then – as the Professor had put it himself – to become an assistant Professor. "That's it!" Mata thought to himself having remembered his future obligations in lieu of firstly finding something to think about on the way to Resavska Street and secondly grasping the reality that his future was brighter than that of perhaps ninety percent of his peers.

It was at that point that the ominous book hidden inside his credenza didn't seem to him to be a bad omen for he didn't know of any bad things that life had in store for him, nay, he began pondering the unthinkable: to share his bound version of the *Levels of Learning* with his Professor. This was a notion which carried him until he had crossed Desanka Maksimović Street still heading towards his destination, but not on the side of the King Alexander Boulevard but rather on the side of Krunska Street. Mata Gradinar simply wanted to avoid the noise and the crush of people on the extremely poorly designed and built Boulevard. It wasn't as if he was losing time, not in the slightest, he was just moving in parallel to the supposed big street which housed, among other landmarks, the freshly restored Metropol Hotel.

He wanted none of that, so when he finally got to the No.3 streetcar stop, Mata Gradinar found no one there even after – having checked his wrist watch – he made sure he was on time.

Mata's first reaction to such tardiness on the part of his friends and especially on the part of the main organizer of the whole shindig was to call Alma Malarosa and give her a piece of his mind, when he saw a completely empty streetcar coming his way from its Tashmajdan roundabout which was its starting point, the starting point of the No.3 line.

"Never before, never again," Mata spoke below the power of voice.

When suddenly he saw on the display above the streetcar's windshield the words "RESERVED TRANSPORT", and when the vehicle pulled up to the station where other people were gathered by now of course, Mata Gradinar learned that he was the only welcomed boarding party.

The driver only opened his front doors and as soon as he did they became shut again and the streetcar was sent on its way with a myriad of cuss words and fists waving in the air on the part of the other passengers who were to remain waiting at the stop for another No.3 streetcar to come along, at least for now.

Much to his surprise, and seated way back in the streetcar were all of his friends. Their shouts of "Happy birthday" rang out amidst the bell disseminating the news of joy on the part of the driver, for which – don't kid yourself – he was handsomely paid.

After the kissing and the hugging had subsided and Mata Gradinar had expressed his truest thanks without having to fain enthusiasm, for he was never given a birthday present like this one, they all took their places as day slowly turned into a dusky hue. The streetcar pressed on doing so very slowly down Resavska Street when Alma Malarosa approached the driver:

"You're not to make any more stops until Miloshev Konak, correct?"

"It's your ride, mam. Agreed," the driver replied.

Having reached the Army Barracks, they turned right towards the Central Train Station behind which the Bus Terminal was dispensing with its vehicles every which way across Serbia. Their streetcar halted on the traffic light with all of the parties who were invited to Mata's birthday seated in a coupled-up fashion: Alma was sitting in Mata's lap, Neli was sitting in Oli's lap and Gabriela was sitting in Erroneous's lap.

Having gotten the signal to move forth, the streetcar headed left or, more precisely, to the west and into the dusk now already visible in Savska Street through which they were headed. As agreed the driver didn't make any stops, but then again he wasn't speeding in his driving which made the ride for all those present all the more pleasant while they watched the people outside waiting at the No3. streetcar's stops spread their arms in disbelief for it was a Friday and everyone was anxious to get home as soon as possible. They were headed straight towards Bonobo Hill but in fact that wasn't to be their final destination. The driver pressed on the button in his cabin and the rails separated at the last moment taking them right through the Northern section of Miloshev Konak, a park very popular but now half-empty due to the time of day with the weekenders.

This was the birthday boy company's last stop. The driver of the streetcar opened his front door and – not to be remiss – Erroneous Petroneus gave him an ample tip. From then on and after the vehicle clunked and clanked its way back towards the station with the company of three couples making their way across the park and towards the street which they needed to cross as well for the Topchiderske Noći kafana was on the other side and there were no traffic lights provided by the city fathers, not at this junction of sorts, for the kafana had an entrance for cars but none for the pedestrians.

Above their heads the Northern star was shining bright as if to make their crossing easier. At one point Mata set foot on the tarmac and the others did follow, finding themselves on the other side of the street of which they knew not the name, all they knew was that they'd left Miloshev Konak and found themselves before the very entrance of Tochiderske Noći kafana.

There was only one more obstacle to overcome and it was one in the shape of an old black dog sound asleep on the welcome mat of the kafana. They saw a face in the side window which overlooked the entrance, it was the face of the proprietor of the establishment and he simply gestured them inside in a fashion which they interpreted to mean that the dog was harmless and that they should simply step over him which they did.

As always and being so far from the city the kafana was not full, quite to the contrary, they were the only ones there which – coupled with the interior of the place – felt to them as if they were in a Stanley Kubrick cadre. It didn't take them long to find a suitable table and give their orders on the beverage of choice which was, in every instance, mulled wine, to the proprietor. Apparently the Topchiderske Noći kafana didn't get many visitors which made their host all the more friendly and cheerful at the sight of new patrons.

Of course, Alma Malarosa had ordered Branko's tort to be made and served in advance, naturally waiting for her cue which came soon after and the entire company, all except Mata Gradinar, stood up and sang "For he's a jolly good fellow" and "Happy birthday" to their friend who was now far away from his previous thoughts. Mata blew out all the candles, well at least the two of them, and the company commenced with the gorge and infusion on Branko's tort and the sweet, mulled wine served, of course, with little carnation flowers.

17

··············· ❧ ···············

The night had engulfed the evening when he got home, and the sun hid the moon out of courtesy for its being tired and weary. Mata Gradinar woke up just in time to bear witness to the sunrise when it dawned on him that there was no more postponing of the obvious, the making use of the book still hidden inside of his credenza. And so, regardless of it being Sunday, he went into the bathroom, showered and shaved and behind the mirrors of the medicine cabinet hanging on the wall half covered in vapor he got out the key to his best kept secret, well best kept as far as he could've trusted Erroneous Petroneus. Then, just in case he needed to go out later to the Farmers Market to get some food, he got dressed (jeans and fine shoes and all) and began folding up his bed into a spacious couch again.

He hadn't spend the night with Alma Malarosa because she had needed the little of what was left of the weekend to practice her graduation play at the Academy for Dramatic Arts and he had abided her with the respect of a gentlemen. But before doing anything rash, having made his bed into a couch, he set about making himself a cup of coffee and breakfast which consisted of two buttered pieces of toast bread which he ate untoasted. We all have our morning quirks and this was one of Mata's. Breakfast he did, but this time not at the kitchen counter as was his practice, but on a tray in front of the TV set watching the early morning programs with pen and paper ready to write down anything and everything which he might want to put in the book. What he was on the lookout for was any kind of affairs at any level of government. He watched and listened to anything which he could compose in a simple syntagm or a name of an institution not knowing himself what would become of it.

His downstairs neighbor was, as custom would have it, playing his acoustic guitar for a little while. Mata tolerated such transgressions against his morning routine because the neighbor in question was an elderly man who made his ends meet by giving guitar lessons to young children. The man's name was Yanisha Paroshki and he lived alone seeing how his wife passed on some years ago. All Yanisha Paroshki had were his pigeons in the open skylight of the building which he would feed corn almost every morning.

Regardless, as Mata was chewing on his breakfast, his bread softened by the fact it had spent the night in the refrigerator there was news coming to him by way of the TV before him of yet another Teachers Union strike. Naturally he put down his tray of food on the coffee table and lunged at the credenza, unlocking it and taking out the book which was as if it were simply waiting for this moment to arrive. Mata Gradinar then returned to sit in front of the television, took a pen from the nightstand which was right next to the phone and turned to page one of the *Levels of Learning*. He didn't know what was going to happen, if anything – he thought – *what if the book were to serve some devious purpose of its maker Mr. Fahmor.* But he felt for some odd reason that he had no time to waste and immediately wrote words down, doing so under the first heading "MINISTRY FOR EDUCATION". The first few seconds nothing happened and those were the longest seconds of Mata's life and then the page on which he had begun writing held true to the first words the book ever yielded which were, "Have it answered".

Column after column, the No.1 page filled with all the relevant information starting with the private data on the current Minister for Education Emilia Tzvetjan and all her private information. Literary everything was listed: from how many sick days she took upon accepting the post to her involvement on other Boards and at other functions which went clearly against the sixth amendment of the Republic of Serbia Constitution which dealt with Conflict of Interest.

Reading down the list, Mata Gradinar couldn't believe that she was also involved with Unionia Bank, the very place Erroneous worked. No wonder his best friend wanted him to ask the book about Unionia Bank. But Mata dared not go any further, he simply remained seated with the book opened in his lap and stared at the TV set. It took the page some time to fill out with all the pertinent information and it was only then that Mr. Gradinar learned that Mrs. Emilia Tzvetjan worked as an Emeritus Professor at his very own Pedagogical Faculty at Belgrade University, which was only one of the functions she had occupied within – let's call it – her area of expertise.

As the morning news continued, Mata Gradinar remained firmly seated at the coffee table staring at the television, and what was odd to him in all this writing down business was that he didn't find it strange. The only major problem was what was he to do if this were to continue. To whom was he to hand over the book once it was all over and done, filled out to the last page with pure, delicious information on anybody be it a person or an institution which might catch his attention. After a short commercial break the morning news continued. This time there was talk about corruption of the judiciary branch of government. Mata Gradinar had no delusions, without so much as listening to the TV he simply turned the page and in the upper left empty field he wrote, in freehand mind you, "HEAD OF THE MERCHANT COURT"

The entire country knew that this was the most corrupt Court of Law in the country, and Mr. Gradinar was anxious to find out what would be the yield of putting them in his book. Among the obvious information which he already knew, there popped out one name, and it was the name of the President of the Court, one Korup Malešević. Mata hoped that he had hit another mark,, and that the book would tell him more about the judge, and he wasn't disappointed. But curiously enough, the book did mention – and this was all in black and white – that Mr. Korup Malešević had dealings, or rather his Court had dealings, with the Unionia Bank. Suddenly there was a fear on the part of Mata that Unionia Bank had its tentacles in most if not all of the institutions in Serbia and it was then that he decided to stop asking the book for answers, fearful that someone would knock on his door too soon. Because, as he figured, "If I'm in a position to obtain this information, who's to say someone else isn't in the know of what I'm doing?" So he stopped immediately for he saw in front of him, right on the morning news program, a police officer, and he grabbed a piece of paper from the nightstand writing down the following question he had for the book that concerned the Minister of the Interior, or, as Mata Gradinar had written it down, the Ministry of the Interior.

Before the morning news was over he put away his book in the credenza below the TV set and retired its keys into the bathroom medicine closet for now. He felt an overwhelming urge to talk to someone about what had just happened to him and that someone, in his mind, needed to be firstly and lastly Erroneous Petroneus.

18

⁓

Allowing him such access must come with a price, Mata Gradinar thought in reference to his *Levels of Learning*. With only moments passing, he took the book out from its hiding place again and shoved it under his arm with the title cover facing his body and left the apartment in such a state that none but his closest friends would recognize him. He was headed for Erroneous's place and was only hoping his friend would be alone that morning it being how he was about to pay him an unannounced visit. He was hoping to catch him on his own with no Gabriela there for he knew that the bakery opened early on Sundays as well. Mata Gradinar didn't have the cash to spread out for a taxi otherwise he would've surely chosen that option, so instead he hopped on the No.25 bus hoping to get to Kumodrashka Street as soon as possible.

Not having to wait long, he saw a bus taking the final curve before its bus stop jam packed with people, there was only one problem with this, only three buses had a stop right there across from the Threshing Floor: the No.25; No.25L and No.26 buses, so he was sure that there would be an onrush to board this particular Public Transportation vehicle. However no such thing happened. And to wit he noticed something strange as well: people were looking at his book as if he was carrying a relic of sorts or a witch's spell book, as if he was some kind of profit of doom. *Perhaps*, Mata thought, *that was why the majority of people were standing well away from him.*

What he didn't know; not having finished watching the morning program on TV like most of the people on the bus stop had, was that Mr. Korup Maleshević had appeared on the morning program live and voiced his fears about some of the most important dockets of the Merchant Court which had been put ad acta and were now missing. Be that as it may, Mata Gradinar boarded the bus along with a happy few who had waited long enough for their ride to come round. He took out his Bus-Plus card and swiped it across the readout screen as the vehicle got going. Once the doors closed their driver was off to the races. Truly it was so, it was as if he was in some weird bus racing championship, the only ones he would let pass in front of him were the pedestrians going to and coming from the Market. The driver knew that his was the highest of responsibilities, to tend to the safety of his passengers.

Having passed the Maxim Gorki Street and come onto the junction between it and the South Boulevard, the bus driver put the bus into first and continued straight up the hill, from then on it was 'hold on for your dear life.' At that point and having made a few more stops, Mata Gradinar gave his seat to an old lady who had come up with what was obviously the perfect method for finding a seat in a full bus – she would talk the person sitting to death.

Coming down from the hill, the bus came onto Ustan-ichka Street and after making one more stop continued straight towards the highway overpass taking a sharp right-turn towards a number of small, meandering streets in order to get to Kumodrashka Street where Mata Gradinar got off the bus.

There he got out his Cell phone and dialed Erroneous Petroneus at his home.

"Are you alone?" Mata asked.

"Yes. Are you really here already?" Erroneous asked.

"Yes. Is Gabriela there?"

"No. Tish just left for work."

"I'll be right over."

"Did you bring the book?"

"Yes, and you're not going to believe what's going on."

"Oh, I believe. You didn't see the morning news in full this morning, did you?" Erroneous asked.

"No, but I have a sneaky suspicion that something has gone awry."

"Just you come by."

"I'll be right there," Mata said.

Mr. Gradinar made his way through the neighborhood and finally found Erroneous's place. Luckily for Mata he saw that Erroneous had the air conditioner running, otherwise he would have had to breathe in all those smells of loveforging Mr. Petroneus and Ms. Tishma most probably did last night. He came to Erroneous's front door and pressed the button on the intercom.

"Who is it?" Mr. Petroneus asked.

"What do you mean 'who is it?' It's me, Mata."

"What's the books password?"

"'Have it answered.'"

"Okay, come in quickly."

It was all so silly, you see, for Erroneous's apartment was on the ground floor, therefore anybody who was awake and having

their coffee on the terrace – and his building had many terraces
– could've heard what they were saying in order to conceal, what
was obvious to any neighbor in keeping with the tradition of
eaves dropping – which was probably as old as the Romans –
their secret of some sorts.

Mr. Petroneus buzzed him in and with a rush to his step Mr.
Gradinar found himself standing at his best friend's front door
– he rang again.

"Do you have a Coke?" Mata asked having dropped the
book too leisurely on the coffee table, "I'm parched. It's so hot
this morning, I could have sworn that the bus driver was driving
so fast just so that he could get some wind in his face."

"You're still afraid of riding the Public Transportation
vehicles?"

"No, just those damn buses and trollies. But most of all
buses, especially when they're making those sharp turns and I
think that the driver hasn't slowed down enough to make it and
that the whole bus is going to tip over…"

"Here, here, here's your Coke, nice and icy cold."

"Thank you. You really are a good friend. Now let us take a
look at our little baby," Mata said talking about the book sitting
on the coffee table.

"I'd rather not get involved, so don't call it "our" anything,"
Erroneous said.

"You do realize that everything that I've written in the book
has come up connected to your Unionia Bank. Shall I ask the
book about the bank or shall I leave it alone?"

"Have you no fear, Mata. Don't you realize that everything
you inquire within the book goes out into the ether, i.e. into the
airwaves?" Erroneous said in desperation and fear for his friend.

"So I'm well protected, am I not?"

"How do you figure?"

"Well, if everybody knows than no one is none the wiser. The fact that it's burning under their feet wouldn't exists if it wasn't for the other fact."

"And what is the other fact?"

"That they've done something wrong. And by the way, has any reporter so far come out with the source for their news stories; any at all?" Mr. Gradinar asked.

"No, not publically, anyway."

"Then I'm in the clear. Besides, I consider this to be my public duty."

"Yes, well, that's just the problem you're not a public official. You haven't or aren't ever going to be part of the official system."

"That's not the point."

"Do tell then, what is the point?" Mr. Petroneus asked.

"Anything man can use he can abuse. That's the point. And this book serves to ensure that as little of that goes on in our society."

Luckily for the two of them the windows and the door to the terrace were closed due to the air conditioner being on, otherwise who knows who might have heard them talk no matter how farfetched their theories were. Talking together it became clear that Erroneous Petroneus was of a mind to let things remain as they were, Mata Gradinar not so much, he wanted not control but to initiate actions towards the positive. His creed quickly became one of the ones repeated throughout history: "Get them by the balls and their hearts and minds will be forced to follow."

19

Mata's visit to his friend provided him in with a lull in activity in which he tended to his new job at the Pedagogical Faculty and his first meeting with his former Professor Neven Goryan. Up until his meeting with the Professor Mata Gradinar didn't perceive his graduate paper as a caveat of sorts, but nevertheless he did feel as though he had taken a slice of life which wasn't his for the taking, and that being thus regarding that Sunday, the first thing he decided was to return home and put the *Levels of Learning* away and wait for tomorrow and his big meeting. He couldn't help but feel small due to the boldness with which he had talked about the book of which even Erroneous had washed his hands. Who did he think he was, anyway? He was a simple graduate student up until yesterday and now all of a sudden, upon getting a slice of power – or in the least that's how Mata interpreted his book – he was himself becoming corrupt. For what is information if it's not in the hands of an ethically enlightened and most of all loyal professional, which was something Mata Gradinar surely wasn't, it's nothing more than a tool with which to influence and with

which to put others – men and women in the halls of power
– under his thumb without ever breaking any legal norm ever
written for it was, or at least it seemed to Mr. Gradinar, that he
was the one writing them.

How many times had humanity tried and failed in patch-
ing up all of the discrepancies and shortcomings in its various
– no matter the variability – systems and failed, failed in the
long run of course. And suddenly here comes this kid out of
nowhere with a damn book no less and everybody was supposed
to adhere; no what Mata Gradinar should've and indeed did feel
was fear, fear for his own safety. It was precisely out of that fear
that he didn't continue writing in his book regardless of the fact
that he knew exactly what he wanted to write down, or as the
book itself so invitingly asked "Have it answered", and that was
in capital letters "THE MINISTRY OF THE INTERIOR".

No, not even a person who made all the dockets disappear
from the corrupt Merchant Court, as he saw stated by its president Korup Maleshević, and have them transcribed into the book
for his reading pleasure was dense and dumb enough to charge
at the Ministry of the Interior, not yet anyway. Mata Gradinar
knew, well he had no way of actually knowing, but he portended
that the police were already working on the case of the missing
Court dockets, so he held back from further provocation decid-
ing not to write anything more into the book but instead to read
what had come from his writing so far.

His television was off letting silence reign supreme throughout his apartment. He didn't need to unplug or switch off his
phones for he knew that no one would call for it was his experience that rarely was he the recipient of any such phone calls,
rather instead he was the initiator of get-togethers and reunions,
meetings and such. In such a pleasant silence, while reading up

on the biographies in his special book – very much personal
biographies – of Emilia Tzvetjan (the Minister for Education)
and Korup Malešević (the President of the Merchant Court,
and the biggest fish he had caught so far), Mata Gradinar was
interrupted by his neighbor's very loud guitar playing. As told
previously, the man's name was Yanisha Paroshki and he lived
one floor right below Mata Gradinar. He was hard of hearing
but refused to wear a hearing aid even though he had long, gray
hair which would have hidden his narcissism very well, but he
wouldn't hear of it – no pun intended.

As the playing from below continued, Mata Gradinar had
finally had it and decided to go down to his place for the first
time. You see, up until now Mr. Paroshki and Mr. Gradinar had
an arrangement which consisted of Yanisha allowing Mata to
bang on his floor wherever he, Yanisha, would make too much
noise. But this time there was so much noise that Yanisha Paroshki couldn't hear his, Mata Gradinar's banging on the floor
with the ten kilo weight he used to exercise. Naturally Mata put
the book away in the credenza, locked it and headed for the
bathroom where – in the medicine cabinet – he deposited the
aforementioned key to the greatest treasure he's ever held in his
possession.

Mata then proceeded down the stairs and to the front of the
aging man's door. He rang the bell but the guitar was still playing something on which the piper has long gone collected, i.e.
it was the music from the moth ball bags of yesteryear. And yet
Yanisha Paroshki still couldn't hear a thing, so Mata, who knew
the song the old man was playing, waited for the beak in the riff
and again banged against the door.

Yanisha opened, he looked worn out but not tired; his hair
was – for no apparent reason – all disheveled and he looked like

a porcupine. Mr. Paroshki didn't have an angry expression on his face as one would expect from a genius whose skill of concentration was broken by a nuisance of sorts. No, there was nothing like that about the man who was now inviting Mata, who had just caught him in a pause, to come in during a break he was planning to take before another one of his students came along.

"Mister Paroshki, didn't you hear me beating the hell out of your ceiling?"

"No, my hearing is very poor. You see I look for when the chandelier begins to move and rattle, that's how I know that I'm bothering you with my music."

"Tell me: How long have you been playing the guitar?"

"Oh, forever. That is until my hearing began to go. Hang on I'll get us some beers, everybody likes a cold one," Mr. Paroshki screamed from the inside of his kitchen.

Upon his return with the drinks, the two men began discussing what was going on in the news. And while there were mostly domestic affairs it didn't keep them away for waiting for the news to come on the television. Finally when the beer cans were half empty and when Mr. Paroshki lit up his cigarette, there she was as large as Yanisha's TV screen would allow, the Minister for Education holding a press conference in which she gave her resignation to that post having said that the matter had already been discussed with the Prime Minister and that he supported her in her actions.

"It works. Its writing history itself!" Mata Gradinar shouted forgetting his place in the matter.

"Ah-a, but it's not history when a Minister hands in her resignation. Where's the affair behind that. Besides, all she stated was that her resignation was for private, personal reasons."

"Don't bet on it, sir."

"What do you mean?"

"It's only a matter of asking the right question. The trouble with that is how does one copyright a question, you know, for one's own personal protection.

"Maybe I'm hearing you wrong, Mata… Are you saying that you have something to do with this resignation of one of our Ministers?"

"No, of course not. I think most of us have much better things to do than to worry about the fate of otherwise overpaid politicians."

"I'll drink to that," Yanisha Paroshki said as he lifted his can of beer.

The host's intercom went off and there was a child's voice asking to come in for his guitar lesson.

"Don't worry;" Yanisha said to Mata, "you'll get your peace and quiet now. These kids today know nothing about the guitar. In fact, why don't you stay, it'll cheer you up. I know I always get a kick out of it, especially when it is they that pays for the lesson in the end."

"I'll stay on the condition that you buy a hearing aid," Mata Gradinar said half-joking.

"No way."

"Why are you so quick to dismiss?"

"Because of the lessons. Why would anyone pay an old has-been like myself good money if they knew I was going completely deaf?"

"Fair point. With that I'd better be going. I hear your students footsteps on the stairwell."

"Suit yourself, it would be a free concert of sorts."

"Do you have any kids who actually have talent for the instrument?"

"Yes there is this one boy. In fact, I'll let you know so that you could come and watch us work. Well, watch him work; because I tell you, I have nothing more to teach him and it would be excellent company to listen to.

"Meanwhile I have to play nice and be supportive and understanding of these other talentless hacks."

"I would very much like that, Mister Paroshki, very much so."

"Then it's done, settled until next time?"

"Yes is is, goodbye, good sir."

"Goodbye, Mata."

As Yanisha Paroshki was showing Mata to the door, it now flung well open, and there was a sight of a boy dragging behind him along the floor what couldn't have been mistaken for anything other than a guitar case. Though well-off, the child looked ridiculous, unlearned and horribly stupid.

20

As soon as he realized it was still Sunday, Mata Gradinar decided to proceed to 27th of March Street to catch the No.65 bus to New Belgrade and visit his Alma Malarosa at the Academy of the Dramatic Arts. He had heard through their mutual friends Oli Uzdlak and Neli Nizdlak that she was brilliant in a not so brilliantly written play which her class was preparing as their graduation piece. But Mata didn't worry, especially after seeing her toothpaste commercial in which – as he had thought and always will – Alma was phenomenal, particularly when she told him that they shot the commercial in one take.

It was still the morning hours, perhaps nine, perhaps sometime around ten o'clock when he boarded the designated Public Transportation bus. But whatever the time was it was certainly looking like a lazy hour. People were slow to move and – as if by protest – nobody wanted to sit down, they all placed themselves below the roof windows of the bus in order to cool their bodies from the morning heat. This was, of course, no skin off Mata Gradinar's hide who – having checked his Bus Plus card – sat down right by a window through which the sunlight was scorching its way in. Luckily for the driver, the rout wasn't a difficult one, and all he had to do, as far as it concerned Mata, was get them over Branko's bridge to which the city fathers have recently given a fresh coat of blue paint in keeping with the tradition of that particular bridge's color.

And as all of the above began coalescing in what was to be Mata Gradinar's last stop in the New Belgrade part of town, he readied himself to get off the bus which he did right across from the Grawe Insurance building, leaving the Public Transportation Vehicle to proceed to Bežanijska Kosa (which we won't get into). He could've taken a different bus if he wanted to continue in haste, but Mata Gradinar decided to make a day of it, besides he hadn't seen the old married couple of Neli and Oli since their last get-together. That being as it was, he hoofed it on foot through the intersecting boulevards of New Belgrade. He was in awe of how much space these people were provided with. There was a lot of jealousy brewing inside of him in a much more profound way that it would in a usual observer who – let's say – lived there in New Belgrade.

What Mata liked the best was asking the natives of New Belgrade (otherwise known as The Dormitory) where was and how could he get to the Academy of the Dramatic Arts. Everyone he had approached had a different answer, and as it turned out everyone's answer was correct but for the different geographical position of Mata Gradinar and any particular stranger from whom he would ask for directions.

Then, as if a building straight out of Oscar Niemeyer's Brasilia, he finally found the Academy, the façade of which was covered in spray paint drawings and other types of graffiti. Once it had bolstered a surrounding made up entirely out of sand

dunes, but now, with all the colors, it was made to look some-
what fancier. There, Mr. Gradinar went in but there was no one
there, not a single soul. The glass box at the very entrance usually reserved for security was vacant and it had a perfect, round
bullet hole in it.

What could have done that? He made his way through the
main corridor of the ground floor in the search for his Alma
Malarosa when, much to his fortune, he saw Oli Uzdlak coming
out of one of the doors behind which hid his Alma. So as not to
raise alarm by screaming, Mata summoned Oli with the taping
of his shoe heels against the marble floors and raising his hands
so that Mr. Uzdlak, who's approximation was farther than Mata
had surmised, could spot him, which he did.

"I've just come out for air," Oli Uzdlak said to Mata who
was standing there next to him.

"Is the room not air-conditioned?"

"It's not that, Mata. It's the play."

"What about the play?"

"It stinks. So there."

"What are you saying, that my Alma is embarrassing herself?"

"No, of course not."

"Than what is it?"

"She is the only one who can salvage that carcass someone
decided to put on paper," Oli Uzdlak said.

"But she's starring in it, isn't she.

"I told you, don't worry; Alma Malarosa is the only bright
spot in the entire shambles and charade."

"How can I not worry?"

"And why should you?" Oli Uzdlak asked unwittingly.

"Don't you know who'll be on the premiere of her graduate
performance?"

"Who?"

"Producers, agents, directors. You name it."

"I hadn't thought of it that way. Oh, now I get it…"

"Get what?! Speak up!" Mata Gradinar was growing inpatient.

"Shh, keep your voice down."

"Well speak to me then or at least drop me more hints if you seek to keep your opinion to yourself."

"That's why she worked her Shakespeare joke into her part."

"And the Professors allowed it?!"

"Naturally, my boy. Who wouldn't," Oli Uzdlak said.

"Heaven help me, this means that she knows she's in trouble and is trying to get out of it."

"What makes you say that? You know, maybe you should be the one on stage, what with your being so dramatic and all."

"Don't you see, and trust me on this, I know my Alma, if she's bringing in new material, a joke of hers, into the play…"

"But, Mata, the Professors have approved all that she's done so far. If anyone is going to flunk it'll be the person who wrote the cursed thing."

"The person who wrote the cursed thing," those words of Oli Uzdlak stuck in Mata Gradinar's mind and he immediately thought of his book lying safely in the credenza in his studio apartment.

"Right, right. Can we…, I mean would it be okay if I come in to see what is going on inside with you?"

"Of course. And I'm sure that Alma would love to see you up in the sparse but very much chosen audience. You know that my Neli is here too, yes?"

"It didn't escape my notions of suspicion that Missus. Nizdlak might be here," Mata said.

"Trust me, my friend, if things keep progressing between you and Miss Malarosa in the present fashion, you'll be in the same situation."

"Oh, Oli, I don't create situations, I make them go away onto another."

"Good, I'm glad to hear that. Now close the door quietly as you enter."

Inside, both the voices on stage and those sitting in the front rows were awry. The young man who wrote the play was an arrogant prick which was an assertion Mata made based on his constant bickering with his Alma Malarosa. While sitting in the dark Mata naturally said hello to Neli Nizdlak who had a look about her countenance that she wanted to leave this place for it seemed – the practice that is – would from the looks of it go on forever. And while the playwright-wannabe argued his points of contention with the Professors solely on the esthetic bases, Alma put up her resistance based on what she had learned at the Academy so far in regards to the craft of acting. There was a great deal at stake and they were all butting heads.

It seemed to Mata that it was going nowhere. Those who were in the audience comprised mostly of friends who were beginning to leave the auditorium one by one and later on in droves. Finally, in order to salvage his Alma's natural inborn talent, Mr. Gradinar simply yelled out:

"Why don't the players go through it once with no interruption!"

He wasn't shy about it, hell; he was standing as he shouted those words with which everybody agreed. And so the play was run through once again, this time as a whole and when the future actors were done Mr. Gradinar saw the playwright approach the

Professors with his head bowed and manuscript in hand whispering the words: "I'll rewrite it."

See, words of truth are not always shouted from the rooftops, but sometimes from the balcony.

21

By the time the young, aspiring actors-to-be were finished performing their graduate play – the one about to be rewritten – Mr. Gradinar, who suggested the repeat, was asked by the Professors to leave the room with the words: "No audience participation, please."

Many got up and left right along with him for reasons he didn't understand, including Oli Uzdlak who was only later joined by his wife Neli Nizdlak in the corridor of the ground floor of the Academy. The Academy itself was built – much like the rest of New Belgrade – in the style of Social Realism which meant it had function above all other aspects of the structure.

"Why did you have to shout?" Neli asked cross with Mata.

"Do you prefer watching a patchwork being torn apart or an entire play? Why do you think I shouted?" Mata replied.

"Please, do tell," Neli pushed for the answer.

"To see the entire play, that's all the reason I can give," Mata gave his answer.

"What does he mean?" she asked as she turned to her Oli. "What do you mean by that?" she asked Mata.

"I think what he means is that he wanted to see Alma perform. Am I right, Mata?" Oli interjected sensing a prolonged argument.

They kept their voices low so as not to be heard by others in the corridor comprised mostly of the elderly relatives and eager parents and grandparents of student actors they could hear practicing from within.

"Oli is absolutely correct. Why did they organize an open class if they didn't want constructive criticism? Besides, none of the Professors know who I am so I can be certain that likewise none of the blame for the perceived interruption will fall on her part, do pardon the pun but we are at the Academy," Mata answered.

"So now, because of you, I can't see my best friend do what she does best?!" Neli said to Mata.

"Who told you that you must leave the heater?" Mata asked.

"Well…, no one. It just felt uncomfortable seeing how you and I were seated next to each other."

"So?"

"So naturally I felt obliged to leave after the two of you did," Neli said.

"You're being ridiculous. Go back in and finish watching Miss Malarosa if you so desire," Oli suggested.

"And be gawked at by everyone here! I think not," she spoke with a hint of dread in her voice.

"I really think you should listen to Oli."

"Oh really now?"

"Really?" Oli was a bit surprised by this as well.

"Okay. But only on the condition that you come back in with me," she said to Oli.

"Okay."

"And let's be quiet about it. That means you too, mister! Not a peep until we're well behind this door," she said to Mata Gradinar.

"That's fine by me. I have other things on my mind anyway, but don't say that to Alma, I don't want her to be upset."

"You have our word."

"Good, I'll wait for her here. Besides, I think that one of the Professors got a good look at me and that my coming back in wouldn't pass without a scandal of some sorts," Mata said.

"You see. Now you're getting my point. C'mon, Oli."

When the door was opened by their going back inside the auditorium there was a dead silence, all but for one voice which Mata Gradinar recognized, and that was the voice of the girl from the toothpaste commercial now going through octaves as if it was nobody's business. It was then that he learned – through that brief opening and closing of the auditorium door – that his Alma Malarosa could act with her voice as well. This came as a surprise to him, keeping in mind the astounding physical beauty with which she was endowed as a woman let alone as an actress. He so desperately wanted to go back in but at the same time didn't want to cause any more trouble for his Alma, thus setting up a course for himself to pace over the entire length of the Academy's ground floor corridor. As if on guard duty at a military barracks he minded that his steps not be too firm and loud less he might disturb one of the Professors, therefore jeopardizing his Alma's chances to partake in her generation's graduate performance.

Mata Gradinar knew that he had put to ruin the chance, one which he'll never get back again, and that was to see her act for the very first time. For that to happen – and this he was aware of too well – it would take a professional engagement on her part, and it needed to be something more worthy of her talents than a simple toothpaste commercial. He admired the fact that she wasn't afraid of failure. Mata Gradinar knew – in his pacing up and down that long corridor – that this was a girl who could meet with and solve any problem life might throw her way, and that she thought of nothing as being jettison, not even his graduate paper of which she asked him nothing.

They were exceptionally honest with each other from the moment they met. She immediately told him that she had no interest in pedagogy while he admitted being drawn to the theatrical arts. To any outsider this might seem to resound as her having an upper hand over him, but in fact it was that difference of interests – at least on Alma's side – which drew them together. Luckily for Mata Gradinar Ms. Malarosa didn't pry or was one of those girlfriends who had to know everything about their mates, so his book was well out of the heart and out of mind of his Alma. As far as his *Levels of Learning* was concerned she had asked him only once, and this around the time he was defending his paper, about the whereabouts of the book, hardcopy version of it, to which Mr. Gradinar had replied that he hadn't wanted to spend the money on pure style and something as superficial as taking the text to the bookbinder so he had kept it in his computer files and on his USB stick, and nothing further was said on the matter.

Suddenly the voices of the future actors fell silent behind the door of the auditorium and Mata Gradinar began looking for which one was the door that led to the backstage of the auditorium from which he was so thoroughly thrown out. He took a turn at the bottom end of the corridor but only managed to come across a stairwell there. The only possible point of ingress for him was the last door on the far side of the corridor. Upon stepping inside he immediately realized he had succeeded in his quest to surprise his Alma, the only crux of the matter was that he hadn't bring her any gifts. Mata didn't care that what she just went through was but a rehearsal for the actual play, he simply didn't like meeting up with her under any circumstances empty-handed. Mr. Gradinar imparted these habits and worries to her once the two of them found each other in a warm embrace in what was indeed the backstage of the auditorium.

"How did you find me?" Alma asked.

"I have a confession to make."

"Regarding?"

"It's in light of it being me that was thrown out of your rehearsal by one of your Professors."

"Oh, you needn't worry. That kind of stuff happens all the time. But let me tell you that all my colleagues are happy with what you did back then."

"Really?"

"Yes. We all feel that the playwright is a pain in the neck. Did you happen to see what happened in the end?"

"No, I did not. All I managed to hear was him telling one of the Professors that he'll rewrite the play."

"And that's all that needed to happen, but none of us had the guts to say it because of his connections at the Academy. You, my love, in your request that we run the entire play, brought him down about a dozen of pegs to the point where he considered doing a rewrite."

"I'm glad I could help, even though I did it unwittingly..., but..."

But before he could tell Alma Malarosa that he was in a rush to meet his Professor regarding a job, and that he had to catch any of the following buses: No.65; No.71 or No.71L he found her arms wrapped tightly around his neck and the assault of a hundred kisses landing all over his countenance. Mata Gradinar did eventually succeed in coming around to his obligations after he explained to his love that he needed to catch a bus to Zeleni Venatz or Zelenjak which was also a Farmers Market located across from the many a buses last stop, and from there he would proceed on foot to Queen Natalija Street No.43.

22

⸙

Egregious as the bus waiting was, Mata Gradinar saw that none other was to leave behind New Belgrade in any other manner but via a Public Transportation vehicle yet to arrive because his wallet was bitterly empty for a taxi ride to Queen Natalija's No.43. But unlike the state of his wallet Mata's heart was full of the prior expression of love towards him by Ms. Malarosa and it is in that condition that he boarded a bus and thus quickly finding himself on the Mihailo Pupin Boulevard and from then on it was a straight line across the bridge of blue, across the Sava River and further into Branko's Street whereupon the bus made its final stop for now, right across Zelenjak.

The Pedagogical faculty was right across from the Obstetrics hospital and Mata Gradinar always thought there was a kind of poetic justice to that fact, as in "get them learning while they're young," so to speak but not in such drastic, graphic terms. He found Professor Neven Goryan in his office swamped by papers; graduate papers much like the type Mata's once was. There was a kind of plead for mercy on the Professor's face and a sign of hope as Mata Gradinar walked into his office. Professor Goryan explained the new job to Mata as best he could. Mr. Gradinar's primary role was to assist the Professor in office work – much like the assistance he was so in need at present – secondly Mr. Gradinar was to go over and read as many papers as he could in a day's work and thirdly he was to cater to both his and the Professor's needs as was concerned insofar as coffee and lunches were in question.

Mata Gradinar didn't mind the required work, in fact when he found out about the salary it was all he could do to stop himself from calling his parents from the Professor's office as the money in question was quite sufficient to cover his food and rent needs with a little something to keep to himself. With this he had the feeling that he had finally made it, and as of that day he was – in a manner of speaking – in the government's manger. What interested him the most was the reading of the papers of some of the other students, for among them were names which he knew and studied with, it was just the fact that Mr. Gradinar graduated first and top of his class which made him feel uneasy about that aspect of his job, no matter how comfortable a post he had indeed taken upon himself. First thing was first though: if he was going to work full-time (and he was), Mata Gradinar needed to get a work booklet from the Unemployment Bureau, and to this Professor Goryan was more than happy to oblige.

"Don't worry, my boy, today is Sunday and unlike my office the Bureau is closed. But first thing tomorrow you're to go and get your work booklet. I know it's a hassle but it must be done if we are to take you on full time, and believe me the Dean has very high hopes for you. So promise me you'll do it. Are you on board?"

"I'll be more than happy to work for you, Professor Goryan. Of course, so from tomorrow on it is then?"

"Yes."

"Good," Mata responded confidently.

"You may have a look around. Right there, on that desk, are some of the other graduate papers you're to go over. I'm sure you'll notice your own footprint in the works of your stalling colleagues," Neven Goryan said.

"You don't say?"

"You're either too modest, or too self-involved. I can't decide which at present."

"Oh, Professor Goryan, I don't keep secrets. I don't have the energy for it."

"I beg to differ…"

"Well, if that's the case, then we'll have to disagree," They both laughed.

"Won't you stay a while longer, Mr. Gradinar?"

"No, I'm terribly sorry, but I can't."

"Oh, you've made other plans?"

"Naturally, it's Sunday."

"How I envy you. Everything must come so easy to you, Mr. Gradinar."

"That's because I've made necessity the driving force in my life."

"Necessity, you don't say."

"Well, the Greeks have said it already: 'Necessity is the mother of all innovation,'"- Mata quoted.

"Ha, ha, ha, ah yes, of course!" the Professor laughed with delight.

"My dear Professor, have you ever heard the saying that 'Perfect society will exist only when philosophers become statesmen.'?"

"No, who was it that said that. It's on the tip of my tongue…"

"It was Plato. And our country was perhaps one of the first in modern history to have a chance to test that proposition of Plato's, if only Prime Minister Đinđić hadn't been assassinated."

"Please. Let's not go into politics, shall we?" Neven Goryan looked tired.

"You're right, sir. And I am sorry to leave you with all this work…"

"Don't worry, my boy, somewhere in here there is order. That's why I hired you, to find it. Goodbye Mr. Gradinar."

"Goodbye Professor Goryan."

As was previously stated Mata had no money in his wallet so he decided to walk home and as it was Sunday, thankfully for him – for he was not in the mood – he didn't meet any of his old faculty colleagues neither in or in the vicinity of the building from whence he was departing. He knew he was going to have to work very hard to keep any kind of job with Professor Goryan, but then again, everything seemed to be easy for him to do thus far. Whatever project he would begin he was certain he would finish without a hitch. This was just another opportunity for him to prove his worth firstly to himself and then to the rest.

As he stood at the traffic light at Count Milosh's Street, from across the way Mata Gradinar could swear that he saw none other than Mr. Bleh Fahmor's apprentice coming from work which was obvious a) because of his bearing; and b) because those who worked Sundays were now heading home for it was that time of day. Seeing this Mata wanted to test something out so when the traffic light turned a shade of pedestrian green and the crowd merged and bypassed the individuals in between, Mr. Gradinar made sure he would be just in the right location to be passing by Mr. Fahmor's apprentice and when he did he simply whispered to him below the power of voice:

"Have it answered."

Hearing this, the young man stopped immediately in his tracks while Count Milosh's Street was fast being cleared of pedestrians with the traffic light now blinking in its pedestrian green as a warning sign for any walkabout to clear the street in which the cars were already geared up to go. In time the apprentice ran and crossed to his intended side of the street, he wasn't sure from whence the voice came, though he did suspect it was Mr. Gradinar (for everyone in Bleh Fahmor's workshop had heard about his book by now) but he never saw Mata with his own eyes and even if he had seen him he wouldn't have known what to do and he would probably run away.

When Mata finally returned home thinking that he would immediately retire to his bed, instead he found that the devil didn't give him any time to rest, his mind racing to and fro, so he unlocked the credenza under the TV set to find that the book has grown thicker in volume. In other words and whereas the heading of the Ministry for Education didn't expand as much other than the very intimate details about the Minister's private life and connections with Unionia Bank, a one Emilija Tzvetjan; the heading of the Merchant Court had almost filled out each and every page of his *Levels of Learning*. It was as if the book had taken on a life of its own, not caring even for its master, the young Mata Gradinar, who knew the power which was at his disposal where it was now only a matter of him controlling that power for which he had no background nor was he properly trained to do so. That being thus, he couldn't help but notice a pattern that all these things which he had logged into his book had something to do with the Unionia Bank, but he left alone that particular institution for now because of one major reason: they worked and operated in a private sector while all the other institutions were those pertaining to the levels of government which were public. Besides, Mata Gradinar had no time to waste, it being a very eventful Sunday, one he decided to end with a cool shower, when the appointed hour came for his night-time regime.

23

---- ✺ ----

In the interim it was a ladies trifecta evening at Erroneous and Tishma's place where the three Singinas had gathered. And while he was told to make himself scarce that night, beforehand Erroneous Petroneus was put in charge of the catering the evening which consisted of him procuring some red Italian wine, prosciutto and a well-stocked selection of cheeses. Alma and Neli coming over was the first sign for him to get out and leave the apartment to the ladies. It played out that way because Alma and Nina wanted to get to know Gabriela a little better. And without further ado Erroneous found himself on the street where he wandered through various corners and neighborhoods to which he never paid any attention before that night. His walking eventually led him to the intersection between Krunska and Molerova Street, and for no apparent reason, Erroneous turned having traversed the Krunska Street thus far in the direction of Baba Vishnjina Street in order to get to Njegosheva Street which was famed for its assortment of cafes.

Just as he was making his turn an old Gypsy woman sitting on an empty beer crate smoking a cigarette said 'hallo' to him.

Being a cultured man he said hallo back not expecting anything in return when instead – much to Erroneous's surprise – the Gypsy woman replied:

"Nice work with that title."

"Pardon?!" Erroneous said taken aback.

"You know, the title for your friend's book. What was it again…, a very nice fellow."

"I have no idea what you're talking about so I would wish that you stop.

"Oh, don't worry so. Besides it was on the Bulletin Board."

"What are you talking about? What Bulletin Board, where?" Erroneous was at the end of his wits.

"Right there, in Molerova Street. You just have to cross Krunska Street and you'll see it hanging on the wall on the right," she spoke with confidence.

And just about as Erroneous was going to leap and rush into action to see what the old Gypsy woman was talking about, she stopped him once more but only after a nagging, smoker's cough, the slime of which she then swallowed.

"You're worried over nothing, sir. The piece of paper is gone. Someone threw it into the garbage dump until two persons, a father and a son found it. You see it had rained and when they were emptying the garbage dumps the paper in question got pasted at the bottom and, from what I've heard…" she was about to go on.

"You heard nothing and you know nothing of the matter, so mind your own business."

"Please allow me to finish for I have proof… Now where was I. Ah, yes…"

"Stop! What proof? Is it material or just and simply the ramblings of an old woman?"

"Mind your tongue, sir, when you're spoken to by a true story teller, or rather I should say, a teller of true stories."

"Go on, I apologize," Erroneous said.

"Yes well, now I've lost my thought-thread. Ah, of course, the father and the son. You see it was the son who climbed into the dumpster and there he found the piece of paper. They were going to throw it out because; seeing how they're homeless their primary interest was food…"

"How do you know all this?"

"A word of a good deed always gets around. Anyway, your friend Mata Gradinar paid them a hundred dinars for that piece of paper."

"How do you know Mister Gradinar?"

"He always says hi to me when he passes me by, an absolutely honorable gentlemen and may I add worthy of the respect for that honor."

"Yes, quite… But what is this evidence you mentioned? And who posted the piece of paper containing the title of the book onto the Bulletin Board?"

"Come with me. I think I have the answer."

"Come where?"

"To my home. It's right in that basement across the street."

As the old Gypsy woman rose to her feet, Erroneous saw that one of her arms was crippled because she was holding it completely askew and right up against her shoulder while she led him across and farther down Molerova Street.

Her apartment was dreadful. Erroneous had to cover his mouth and nose for all the smells of foods which she too – on occasion – had to get out from the dumpsters. And yet he couldn't help but wonder how a woman in such an unfavorable social standing come across any sort of real estate to retain as her own.

"You youths and your writing! You'll be the death of us all," she said unlocking her apartment door.

"Or perhaps simply the death of one," Erroneous said when she shut the door behind them. It was only a basement, yes, but at a prime location in the city. Slowly she showed him inside and once in she locked the door as well.

"So, where is this proof you mentioned earlier?"

"Ha, ha. You have no idea how right you were when you said just now 'the death of one'."

"Okay. I suppose I have some time to kill. Enlighten me please."

"It's all about killing for you this evening, sir, isn't it?"

"My girlfriend is having a ladies only night at our apartment so I'm not allowed in."

"Ah, yes, the beautiful Gabriela Tishma!" she exclaimed.

"Madam, how do you know so much about, well, how should I put it...?"

"You mean how am I like some kind of encyclopedia, akin to a kind of memory bank?"

Erroneous froze when she made reference to an encyclopedia, it being a book and all, so naturally he attempted to steer the conversation off topic.

"Yes, well, if it were up to me I'd hook you up to my computer and use you as an external hard drive."

"Sir, all joking aside, do you or do you not want to see the proof which I mentioned. Hold on, I have coffee brewing; won't you stay and join me?"

"If its store bought I won't protest to a cup, and if you can spare some. Yes, I'll stay to see this proof of yours."

The old Gypsy woman hobbled to her kitchenette divided from the rest of the room only by a heavy drape, and returned with two fuming coffee mugs for the two of them. She sat back down opposite Mr. Petroneus.

"A memory bank, you say. I'd care to wager by the looks of you that you work in banking."

"Yes I do in fact. If you must know I work at Unionia Bank."

"Oh, I've heard of Unionia… But I have to admit that I lied when I said I had material proof of my claim in my apartment… Well, not up until now."

"What do you mean?"

"You are the proof, Mister Erroneous."

"How on Earth do you know my name?!"

"Hear me carefully, if you don't help dismantle Unionia and all their dealings it will cost your friend… it will cost him his life."

"What do you mean dismantle? Are you threatening me, old woman?" Erroneous was now standing and surely ready to leave.

"I must apologize for taking up your time. I'm sure Gabriela is waiting for you at home," and the Gypsy woman tapped the wrist of her crippled hand.

Prompted by that gesture of hers Erroneous took a look at his wrist watch and found that it was well past midnight.

"Open this door!" he commanded.

"The choice is yours and yours alone to make, sir. As you wish. Goodbye," she said while letting him pass.

"Out of my way."

Mr. Petroneus rushed out from the basement and as sure as he was that the stench had disappeared there it was in a slight distance and a pedestrian crossing away from him – the Bulletin Board of which she had spoken. He crossed Krunska Street again and truly there it was, hanging on a building wall with a variety of assortments pertaining to printed material.

Anything from a leaflet to a flyer could be found there, but Erroneous couldn't bear this neighborhood any longer and that being thus he turned on his heels and pace, pace took a brisk walk back home with his own words resonating in his mind: "the death of one".

24

———— ❦ ————

Erroneous Petroneus knew he had to warn Mata Gradinar about what he had learned the previous night from the old Gypsy woman. The only problem was that he couldn't find him at home and he certainly didn't want to barge into his pace of work. His Gabriela Tishma had already gone to work and he was left alone to prepare to go himself to the Unionia Bank. He reprimanded himself for not being able to anticipate the possible pitfalls of his and Mata's strange book venture seeing how he was Risk Assessment Manager. Instead Erroneous got himself into the shower. He liked a good spray of scolding hot water on his body in the morning no matter the season of the year, or the air temperature outside. But that morning was particularly hot and he found himself sweating in large beads as he went about shaving in his fume resistant bathroom mirror.

He finished his morning routine and was about to get dressed for work when there was the ringing of his intercom. It was the postman, so naturally he thought nothing of it. He surmised that the postman was probably delivering bills and such, but on that account he was wrong. When Erroneous had his breakfast, he

headed down the stairs and straight to the mail boxes when much
to his shock and chagrin he found an envelope which contained
the seal of the Ministry of the Interior on its upper left corner.
Seeing this Mr. Petroneus was frightened and his fear developed
to such a level that he got out his cell phone and he called Mata
Gradinar. As he dialed his friend's number he thanked his lucky
stars that he was still in the lobby of his building, otherwise who
knows what the people in the street might have thought of such
a conversation, as it was sure to be strange one indeed. First
off, when Mata answered his friends call, Mister Erroneous was
at his wits end, being full of anger and dismay. He called Mr.
Gradinar on the fact that this one must have written down the
name of the ministry inside his original *Levels of Learning*, to
which he received the completely blaze of an answer of "so
what if I did," or something to that effect.

Looking at the time, it was obvious to Erroneous that Mata
was certainly at his job at the Faculty, most probably in Professor Goryan's office, so it was simple to surmise that he wasn't
available for chit- chat. Still, and be that as it may, Mr. Petroneus
insisted that they set up a meeting time in which to explore their
actions further. To tell the truth, Erroneous Petroneus was so
frightened by the letter from the Ministry of the Interior that he
said to Mata that he didn't intend on even opening it until the
two of them meet and could go about doing so on their own.
They decided to meet after their working hours at the Orient
Express bar, the one situated on the ground floor of the Grand
Balkans Hotel. The proximity suited them both well, especially
Mata Gradinar who – at the level and rate he was working –
was being given home assignments by Professor Goryan, not
for lack of discipline but for want of learning on the young and
eager Mata Gradinar. Also during their cell phone interlocked

conversation, Erroneous learned that Mata had also received the same envelope, precisely from the Ministry of the Interior. But when asked by his friend if he had opened it he answered in the negative thus disabusing Mr. Petroneus of holding on to any possibility of it being some kind of a clerical error on the part of the Ministry in question.

After hanging up the phone, Erroneous Petroneus went outside and found that it was sunny, extremely sunny out. The beams from the sun seemed to make everything translucent so he took his envelope and raised it up towards the light, or what was at least the brightest spot in the sky as he was concerned. But looking carefully he could see that the beam didn't penetrate the envelope. And so, for all he knew it could've been a Court summons for jury duty, but then again, why would they send such a thing in an envelope containing the seal of the Ministry of Interior, and not that of the Ministry of Justice?

And as he was about to deposit the envelope into his inside breast jacket pocket when a thunder cloud placed itself into position right above him. Being of the mind that he had taken enough risks for that day, Mr. Petroneus got out his cell phone and dialed for a taxi; the operator on the other line said he would have to wait three minutes. Those three minutes felt like an eternity to Erroneous Petroneus. And in those three minutes he had the misfortunate opportunity to recall the entire evening from yesterday which he had spent with the old Gypsy woman and her tales of his dismantling the Unionia Bank. But finally the taxi did arrive and having given the driver his destination, Erroneous Petroneus settled in the back seat, only saying to the driver the following:

"Take it slow, and take it in stride, if you will."

However and no matter how comfortable he tried to make himself in the back seat of that cab, Erroneous couldn't help but feel the cursed, damn envelope inside his breast pocket. He was thankful, though, for not ending up as a passenger of one of those talkative drivers who would bend his ears for the whole duration of the ride and to no other purpose except to kill time and perhaps their own portion of boredom in their line of work. Sure enough, the driver got him to the Unionia Headquarters just in time for the rain to begin to drizzle. Mr. Petroneus paid the fare and thanked the man who brought him to work in such ease and comfort of silence.

There he went about his morning routine as usual, firstly greeting the morning guard on duty whom he had known for a long time now, well, at least since he graduated and began working at Unionia Bank. Then just as he was about to head upstairs to his office there was heard the sound of men's shoe heels running towards the elevator with a voice repeating:

"Hold the elevator!"

And why not, so Mr. Petroneus obliged his fellow coworker who happened to be completely soaked and once on his floor he could understand why:, as it had began pouring rain outisde as if it was punishment for all those late for work that day. Mr. Petroneus advised the young man, still dripping puddles in the elevator, to go to the cleaning personnel department and to ask for a towel to dry off. To which he got simple a "thank you, Mister Petroneus" in return for his troubles.

But the weather was the furthest thing on his mind. Erroneous Petroneus kept tapping the side of his jacket which contained the envelope just because he was so nervous, and quite frankly because he didn't at all appreciate the nonchalance with which his friend Mata Gradinar had approached their shared predicament. He had hoped that they were in it together, through thick and thin so to speak, but it was obvious to him that Mata was changing somehow. What was once an a bit nervous, shy but respectful young man was now becoming cock of the roost – or at least he was acting the part exceptionally well. While Erroneous Petroneus knew of this change in his friend, he was also wondering whether Alma Malarosa knew of it as well, or at least – for her sake – had foreboded it in some woman's intuition kind of way. And the reason that Erroneous Petroneus was worried about Alma was because she was his guide when Mata Gradinar's state of mind – which could be unfathomable at times – was in question. Whenever there was something about which Mr. Petroneus was unclear of and which regarded his friend, he would consult on the matter with Ms. Malarosa, and now, especially after they had their ladies night at his and Gabriela's place, he felt comfortable in knowing that Alma had told Gabriela about their sharing anything regarding her Mata Gradinar, thus passing the flame of Erroneous's worries about his friend as far as the amount of information he had on him at any particular time onto his Gabriela Tishma.

25

······· ❦ ·······

Mata Gradinar arrived first at their point of meeting, the Orient Express, which was also the bar of the Grand Balkan Hotel. Upon his arrival he ordered a bottle of champagne and two glasses for he wanted to celebrate his first day at work, or in the least as a regular employee. He expected for Erroneous Petroneus to be late because bankers usually work overtime, especially those in the Risk Assessment business. He had brought with him the same envelope from the Ministry of the Interior as Mr. Petroneus had received. It felt to Mata as if they were both back in schools and were about to compare crib notes. After having a glass of champagne all by his lonesome, Mata Gradinar couldn't help – much like the rest of the hotel bar – but hear the panting voice of Mr. Petroneus asking the bartender whether he saw Mata Gradinar come in which the bartender confirmed with a nod of his head and the pointing of his finger at Mr. Gradinar's table. Erroneous thanked the bartender who proceeded to dabble around and fiddle with the television channels on display for the guests to watch, which he stopped doing when a loud, coarse male voice shouted "Leave the game on." But Erroneous didn't care for sports so upon noticing the scruff of Mata's head which was moving up and down as this one was drinking his champagne, he approached his friend with a kind of nervousness and anxiety usually expressed by an individual who perceives himself to be guilty of something. Mr. Petroneus sat down with his friends on the other side of the table.

"What's all this?" Erroneous asked.

"What do you mean? It's champagne, of course. I wanted to celebrate my first day of work today. So…"

"So what?"

"So ask me how it's been."

Mata Gradinar was a bit insulted by his best friend not picking up on the obvious. But that was just him. Ever since he realized the purpose of his book Mata had become self- centered and egotistical to the point where Erroneous could barely suffer being in his company.

"Have a glass, won't you? Let's celebrate."

"Celebrate, you say. Don't you remember the reason I suggested we meet here I the first place?"

"Oh, certainly! The envelopes."

There was a sigh of relief coming from Mr. Petroneus's side of the table as Mr. Gradinar continued, reaching inside his breast jacket pocket.

"I have mine right here with me. Where's yours?" Mr. Gradinar asked.

Erroneous Petroneus was beside himself with shock at how calm and collected his friend was and then he realized that such a condition of him, of Erroneous, was due to him not having the book. On the contrary: he didn't want to compare letters from the Ministry of the Interior with Mr. Gradinar, he simply wanted Mata to make anything inside the envelope disappear.

"Here, here it is," Erroneous said as he took out his envelope.

"This is so exciting. C'mon, have a sip and we'll open them together."

And so they did. Mr. Petroneus was surprised by the quality of the champagne and – upon sticking his thumb underneath the edge of the envelope – he gestured to the waiter.

"What will it be, gentlemen?" the waiter asked politely.

"We would like a bowl of fresh strawberries, please, to go with our champagne," Erroneous replied suddenly brimming with confidence.

"Very well, sir. One helping of our best strawberries coming right up," and he was gone.

"Mata, please don't tell me that you wrote the words "Ministry of the Interior" in your book," the fright returning to Erroneous's voice.

"As a matter of fact I did. And do you know what I found, my friend?"

Mr. Petroneus was too afraid to ask but couldn't bear the suspense, so naturally he proceeded.

"Pray tell. And don't leave out any details."

"Firstly I found out the Minister's name, and all of his private transactions with your company…"

"My company?"

"Yes, your Unionia Bank. I'm telling you, Erroneous, you wouldn't believe how much butter that man has on his head. And now this, the audacity of sending us letters or who knows what at the same time."

The waiter returned with their helping of strawberries, bid them bon appetite and moved on his way.

"Well, we've got the book so what are afraid off?"

"No, you are mistaken Erroneous, I've got the book. And as far as your fears go I contend they are totally unfounded. So I'll open my envelope first and we'll see what happens next."

"Too bad you don't have you *Levels of Learning* here with you, that way whatever this is could be resolved with a stroke of a pen," Mr. Petroneus suggested.

"It's funny that you mentioned that."

"Mentioned what?"

"The book… You see there's one more thing about it."

"What's that?"

"Some parts of it are growing," Mata said.

"What are you talking about? What parts are growing?"

"For one the part about the Merchant Court. You see, the book is constantly being filled up by details of each and every new docket…"

"My god, that's why Korup Malešević appeared on this morning's news!"

"Did he mention the Unionia Bank?"

"What?" Mr. Petroneus asked surprised.

"Unionia, did he mention your bank?"

"No. But I ask you again: did you write anything about the Ministry of the Interior I your book?"

"Some. I was taking notes while watching the news."

"What for?"

"Just in order to get the name of the person in charge of that particular Ministry. I now know that his name is Slava Pendrek."

"I have to stop you there, okay. I need you not to probe deeper into this matter."

"But why not. It's been so much fun. I can get any piece of information on anyone that catches my eye."

"And what do you plan to do with this, so called, information."

"I don't know yet. For now I'm only enjoying it."

"Enjoying what?" Erroneous asked.

"The sheer knowledge that no one knows what I do. All I have to do is take care of the bookbinder; you remember Mister Bleh Fahmor."

"What about him?"

"He brought this responsibility on me without so much as a consult, and I won't stand for such chicanery. He could've at least told me what the purpose of the book is. So I contend that the only thing a master can ruin is his apprentice."

Having stopped with his tirade and on Erroneous's insistence they finally opened their envelops only to find – much to the anticlimax of one Erroneous Petroneus – that they were only issued a warning that spoke in plain ink of their ID cards about to expire. The letters also urged them to tend to this matter up until a certain, designated date in the Police Station located in Božidara Adžije Street. Then they left the Orient Express bar of the Grand Balkan Hotel in a much better mood than they came in, especially Erroneous Petroneus. But once it came to pass that they had to part ways, Mata Gradinar said something which he himself wasn't sure would penetrate the alcohol soaked brain of his friend who heard the following words uttered to him by his friend: "Don't be posting anything on any Bulletin Boards."

So inebriated was he (Erroneous Petroneus that is) that he simply waved off such a notion with the hand which still held the letter from the Ministry of the Interior which was just one of the documents they needed to bring at the designated date to the police station. That being thus, Mata Gradinar dared not leave Erroneous Petroneus on his own for he was too afraid that his friend would lose the letter or misplace it in some other form of drunken fashion so Mata got out his cell phone and dialed Gabriela Tishma to say and explain why he, Mr. Gradinar, had decided that his friend was to spent the night with him together at his studio apartment.

26

The cell phone conversation was met by some reluctance, as one would imagine, on the part of Gabriela Tishma, but seeing how they were about to deal with the police and that bureaucracy was in question, she let her Petroneus off the hook for just that one night so that he may sober up for tomorrow. Still just to air on the side of caution, Gabriela wanted to talk to Erroneous for a minute, and despite all the warnings she received from Mata not to do so, when he finally gave the receiver to Erroneous he began his babbling and spewing words of love and affection for the unsuspecting poor girl who realized right there that she would be spending the night alone. So much for any more champagne at the Orient Express bar in the lobby of the Grand Balkans Hotel, for Mata and Erroneous had to get a move on in order to rest for what they surmised would be tomorrow's heavy duty bureaucratic undertaking concerning their ID cards and the extension of the same.

They woke up the next day with heavy heads and foggy minds. There were no notes to remind them of what the day

had in store for them, none except for the torn envelops with
the seal of the Ministry of the Interior. Finally, and not wanting to alarm Erroneous, Mata Gradinar went to the bathroom
medicine cabinet to get the credenza key. Once he opened the
piece of furniture Erroneous Petroneus was stunned by how
much the book itself had grown, it truly looked as if it were an
encyclopedia. As Mata was about to open the book whose covers looked as curved as a pregnant woman's belly and seemed
they were about to burst at the seams an airplane flew overhead
which startled Erroneous.

"I want to be someplace else."

"Do you recall why we are here in the first place?"

"No."

"And what are these envelopes with these insignia doing in
our possession?"

"No."

"Then give me your ID card," Mata said.

"No I won't give you my ID card. If you want to transcribe
something do it from your own documentation."

"Fine, as you wish. Unlike you I trust my work," Mata said.

"You don't understand, that's exactly my point. That book is
not your work; it is the work of one Bleh Fahmor."

"Well…, I requested and paid for it and therefore I consider
it to be my own.

And with that Mata Gradinar took out his ID card and
wrote his ID number, the number of the card that is, inside the
book. He immediately got an answer in bold writing which read
that the card was to expire today. The book even directed him to
Božidara Adžije Street where – at the police station – he could
take care of everything.

Having seen that there was nothing to it Erroneous voiced off:

"Do mine… Here, here's my ID card, write my number as well."

"Give it here," replied Mata miffed by his former skepticism.

"But make sure you write the numbers in the correct order; we wouldn't want somebody else's information in there now would we."

As soon as he said it there was a flash of the devious streaking across both their faces as they came to realize yet another use for the now well-bloated book.

"See, it says here that your ID card is to expire today as well."

"That's what those letters must've been in regard with."

"Of course they were, what else could they have been?"

"'Of course' he says."

"What of it?"

"Nothing, it's just that you have a tendency to panic."

"But of course I do. Do you realize how I make my living?"

"Remind me again."

"By tending to other people's assets."

"Christ on a cross, one would think that the police letter was posted on some Bulletin Board!" Mata said.

"What did you say?"

"I…"

"No, scratch that, why did you mention a Bulletin Board?" Erroneous was panicking.

"It was a joke. You did attend University, right?"

"Yes."

"So you have seen a Bulletin Board before. I mean, you know what it's used for, right?"

"You shouldn't joke about things like that. I don't like those kinds of jokes."

"My apologies, it'll never happen again. Are you ready; shall we go?" Mata asked unsure.

"By all means, let's go and straighten this ID card business out."

"Yes, that's exactly what will happen," Mata said sarcastically.

"Why? What could happen?"

"Waiting!" Mr. Gradinar said as he raised his index fingers, yes, both of them.

"How do you figure?" Erroneous reciprocated with a question.

"Well, we're going to get our ID card numbers renewed, right? That means we'll be given our designated numbers either by an orderly or by a number dispensing machine. Now, once we get our numbers we'll stand in line for a certain duration of time which is known as waiting. Now, seeing how we've missed the boat on being among the first ones there I'm going to call into work and explain that I'll probably be late coming in today and I suggest you do the same."

"The same! Heck, I'll ask for a day off. I have one coming every month don't you know?"

"I thought you worked in the private sector. What's this business about getting a day off once a month?"

"What private sector? I work in a bank!" Erroneous had an index finger of his own to raise as he picked up the receiver of Mata's phone.

That was the first time since they knew each other that Erroneous Petroneus seemed like a true and natural predator of the business world in Mata Gradinar's eyes. It was as if Mata was getting a glimpse into the wild side of his best friend's true – or if not true than work-related – psyche.

For the first time he saw Erroneous operate in this one's talk with his boss, a Mr. Deda Blam, who obviously played right along with Erroneous's tune, revealing to Mata what an asset and in how high a regard they held his, Mata's, friend at the Unionia Bank, which was a sentiment that brought him to a reasoning of why was – or at least it was how it seemed – why was Erroneous so nervous every time the book was in question. But for now this was only a slight worry on Mata Gradinar's part, and something with which he was going to confront Erroneous only at a later more suitable time, if at all it should come to.

"There, all done. I have the day to myself. Now you call your little school and make good with your Professor Goryan."

Mata wasn't shocked by such words coming from his friend for he realized that he had just come off a phone high in which he managed to accomplish his goal which was to get a free day. As for concerning himself, Mata Gradinar wasn't as fortunate as his friend, but was still as firm and – dare it be mentioned – arrogant with Neven Goryan as Erroneous had been with his boss. Finally he was told politely that if he wasn't to come in today it would be taken out of his paycheck.

It must have been the book. It couldn't have been anything other than their *Levels of Learning* which was giving them such Dutch courage. So Mata put the book away, locked the credenza and stored the key back into the medicine cabinet in the bathroom. Then they were off to pick a number and that's all they knew.

27

⁓

They were both expecting a long, drawn-out line on Božidara Adžije Street but they weren't met with any crowds there whatsoever. The street was quiet and pleasant that morning and both Mata and Erroneous got into the building comfortably only to find Bleh Fahmor waiting in line in front of them, they knew he was there waiting because of the number printed on a piece of paper which he nervously twirled in his hands. He spoke to them:

"You got here early too, ha?"

"Yes, I suppose. But what brings you to the police station?" Mata Gradinar asked.

"I have to renew my ID card," Mr. Fahmor said.

"You to, ha. Well, let me tell you, when that clock right there strikes seven there won't be room enough for a pin to drop in here. It's good that you came early," Mata said.

"I know the procedure, young man. I've gone through it many more times than you."

"How come?"

"Well, it's not just the fact that I'm older. On occasion I've been known to lose or otherwise misplace my ID card and I always end up here," Mr. Fahmor said.

"So far it is pleasant. C'mon, Mata, let's get our numbers. I apologize, Mister Fahmor, in which room do we get our numbers?" Erroneous asked.

"Room four."

"Thank you. Now c'mon, you pity excuse for an early riser," Erroneous said commandingly.

As soon as they both got up to enter room four, the door of room seven opened up and a lady well on in her years and waist line yelled out: Bleh Fahmor!- calling for him to come in for he was next in line.

"I'll be seeing you around, boys," Mr. Fahmor said to our twosome as they were entering room number four.

"If not, I can always find you in the book!" Mata Gradinar said.

That last sentence by Mata really shook Bleh Fahmor to the core because he knew perfectly well of which book the young man was talking and it drove the fear of god into him. That was the fact as it was figuratively. On a much more realistic and practical level Mr. Fahmor's dread was much more founded and grounded in reality for he knew what he had made when he had crafted that book and was now unsure about the young man in whose possession it was. As it was, all three men stood there upon the green linoleum covered floor staring at each other with their hands on the door knobs of their respective doors which they needed to go through in order to proceed and indeed finish with their business for that day, at least as far as the State was concerned. Doing so Mata Gradinar could've sworn that he saw Mr. Fahmor's lips mouth the expression "The key is the function of the lock.", but he did not want to challenge him on that point of his business and he certainly didn't wish to bring into questioning his profession as well as his standing in the bookbinders community, which he supposed existed. On the other hand, and having truly mouthed that famous sentence Mr. Fahmor could swear that he saw Mr. Gradinar jiggling the door handle of the number four room behind the door of which he then heard a roaring shout:

"Next!"

While at the same time there appeared an elderly, well-aged woman behind the door that Mr. Fahmor was waiting at, so to speak, and reprimanded him for having kept her staff waiting.

"You know, Mister Fahmor, we could do this all day," she said.

"Isn't that the point of a good and well established bureaucracy?" he replied.

"We're not bureaucrats, we're administrators. You should know the distinction by now Mister Fahmor. Now get in."

It was Mata Gradinar who had had the last word, for he saw Mr. Fahmor off to his present time destination before entering the room No.4. Once inside something strange happened - the ID cards of both Mata Gradinar and Erroneous Petroneus were already waiting for them. These were not newly issued ID cards, they were their old ones, the ones they thought and indeed had made sure were lost. Somehow Mr. Gradinar wasn't surprised by this, while Mr. Petroneus had to muster his self-control so as not to leap over the counter and hug and kiss (as the older woman said) the administrator behind the counter. But there was only one thing Mata Gradinar wanted to know:

"Excuse me, but would you mind telling us who brought our ID cards back to the police station."

"Not at all. It was a young man claiming to be nothing but a humble apprentice."

"Yes, of course, but did he say where he had found our ID cards," Mr. Petroneus interjected for want of not coming off as ignorant of the entire situation.

"As a matter of fact he did. He said that this was what he had found pasted on a Bulletin Board right at the intersection between Molerova and Krunska Streets."

Erroneous's heart leapt within his chest and it was then for the first time in his life that he actually felt his blood pressure rise to intolerable levels. He could actually perceive the tiny blood cells hitting and banging against all of his blood vessels.

"Are the ID cards damaged? I ask only because our ID cards have a microchip," Erroneous said.

It seemed odd to Mata Gradinar to see his friend in such an overworked condition. It was as if Erroneous was beginning to faint right there on the counter window. Luckily no one else was in the room – citizenry-wise – except the two of them. Once he came to, Erroneous was himself again. He made a remarkable recovery thanks' only to what he had experienced at the old Gypsy woman's home. That being thus he knew that once that entire ID card business was over and done with, he'd have to say and impart the little encounter he had with the old Gypsy woman and the damn Bulletin Board with his dear friend who was standing right there next to him.

"Mam, does this mean that we can go?" Mata Gradinar said.

"Yes. Just don't misplace your ID cards ever again. No one likes to wait, you just got lucky today seeing how there's no line to wait in, but that was a freak occurrence."

"Erroneous!" Mata shouted at his friend.

"What …?" Erroneous was still in the old Gypsy's basement.

"Pick up your ID card and let's leave this place before we run into Mister Fahmor again."

"Right, right, Mister Fahmor. Well, thank you, ladies. Goodbye."

"Yes, thanks and goodbye," Mata said echoing the sentiment.

"Oh, save it and go!" the chief among the administrators said coarsely.

Erroneous didn't like being talked down to – not by the chief administrator – nor by Mata Gradinar, as though he was half drunk, regardless of whether that would be the case later on, for least one forgets they both had been given a work-free day. It wasn't that he thought less of Mata as a friend, it was however the simple fact that – there he was – a lowly Professor's assistant from the Pedagogical Faculty, telling him what, when and how to do thing. For that sensation a lot had to pass through Erroneous's gullet before he could move on from the point which Mata hadn't even noticed, and the bulk of it was pride. After all it was he, Erroneous, who had named the book and it is because of that fact he found it a bit difficult to get over the fact that the book was now in the charge of one Mata Gradinar.

He had learned quite quickly the power of the book for Mata had written down their ID cards numbers in the book and lo and behold, there they were waiting for them just to be picked up by their rightful owners. As things stood, Mata and Erroneous stayed a little while behind the room marked with the number four, eavesdropping by chance to hear whether Mr. Fahmor had departed and having once heard him bid his thank yous and goodbyes and putting his new ID card into his wallet, the two friend opened the main doors and got out of there.

28

It was obvious and with no omission to it that the book was growing beyond any comprehension either Mata or Erroneous had about power which cannot be expressed or exorcised publicly. They of course, as any a young man, sought solace in the company of their better halves of whom they were immensely proud. No one is so proud of a close person that they cannot at the same instance be proud of themselves. Such a simple notion stems from the fact that – while both Mata and Erroneous always considered the book to be a kind of gift for them to dispose of – they knew Alma and Gabriela as persons for whose affection, time and leniency they had to work for and work really hard for – or at least such is always the case in the head of any man.

Whereas in the presence of the book both young men thought that the world was theirs for the taking, in the company of their gentle better halves they were as tame as a couple of teddy bears. But Alma, Gabriela and Neli's life didn't completely evolve around the men in their lives, which is not to say that they didn't love and care and even at times tolerate them, it was just the simple fact that they wanted to do something on their own; to suddenly wake up in another city, all be it in one of those over-advertised capitals. The Singinas had concluded that Belgrade was not anyone's destination but only a stop along the way to some place more permanent. Besides, who would care to spend time in what the Ottomans called "The city of wars". It was official, the three Singinas had decided to go to Sardinia on vacation and they didn't care what their boyfriends might think of such a decision of theirs. It was only Alma Malarosa who showed fear at the thought of leaving Mata Gradinar on his own. She was afraid that he would leave her if she were to depart – even briefly – for a summer vacation.

"And why should you care if he leaves you?" Neli Nizdlak asked her.

"I'm not sure."

"He did see you work, right?" Neli probed deeper.

"Yes he saw me work!" Alma was growing frustrated.

"Then you have nothing to worry about," Neli said.

"Are you sure?" Alma asked.

"Trust me, any man who sticks by a woman's side after seeing her work will remain loyal to her for the end of his days," Neli said.

"You know, there's some truth to that," Gabriela added. "I'll never forget the way Erroneous looked at me while I was working and he asked me out for the first time. It's as if our men get caught in the headlights or something when we are on their minds, I don't know."

"Gabriela is perfectly right "caught in the headlights" but I think that's what a man gets when he sees a woman he likes *working*. It somehow goes against their grain," Neli Nizdlak added.

"And what about when the couple are married? What then, Neli?" Alma wanted to know.

"Then you weigh your pros and cons for doing something that you know your partner will consider to be off-the-wall and not very well thought through. For example: you tell him but with no intention of getting an answer, secondly it is best to do the con list at dinner, yes, cook him a heavy meal preferably his favorite dish and then bring your plans into the conversation. If need be, try to sell yourself by making the ultimate decision look as if he has made it and not you. In other words lead him on during the conversation, lead him on to think that, in the end, it was he who came up with the idea and not you. But I don't think the three of us will have to resort to any manipulation of that sort. I for one simply plan to tell my husband that I'm going to Sardinia for; let's make it two weeks.

"How about you two?" Neli Nizdlak concluded.

"I have no fears of that nature as far as Mata is concerned. We've known each other since high school and I'm sure he'll let me go without going into a hissy fit," Alma Malarosa said.

There was only one gal left who didn't voice off on the subject and that was Gabriela Tishma. In Gabriela's mind the problem was clear. Whereas the other two girls lived with their mates almost on an equal financial keel, that wasn't the case between he and Erroneous Petroneus. There was more disparity between them and if one were to put the fact that they've been living together for only a brief amount of time and at Erroneous's apartment at that one could see how this made Gabriela feel small. For this reason and much to the shock of the other two she replied:

"I can't go to Sardinia with you."

"What are you, his house wife?" Neli said immediately up in arms.

"Oh, do be quiet for once," Alma said to Neli.

"But look at her. Let's not kid ourselves. Gabriela, you're the most beautiful among us. You have to come to even things out," Neli said standing firm while trying to lighten the mood.

"I won't go. Believe me I'd like to get away for two weeks, but you know how it is in this town: if you're gone a day then you're off the payroll. It's not as if I work in a highly specialized field. I don't want to lose my job, that's all."

"Oh, you poor thing, you're not afraid of losing your job. You're afraid of losing Erroneous," Neli said it.

"That's not fair," Alma interjected.

"No, no, hear me out. I think that our little Gabriela has grown accustom to the everyday routine of her, more or less sheltered life with Mister Petroneus and she doesn't want to challenge him on any account or even a point of fact that a modern-day woman needs time for herself as well as for the man in her life," Neli lashed out because she thought that she had found out the truth.

"You're out of line, Neli," Alma said standing in Gabriela's defense.

"No, unfortunately she's not out of line; she's spot on. I am afraid of losing him. He is better educated than I am, he has a better paying job than I do, and my good looks won't last forever. But please don't take this the wrong way, I do truly love him. But for the life of me I could never ask him such a thing," Gabriela said her shoulders shaking.

"Wait, what thing would you never ask him?" Neli wanted to know, asking in an apologetic tone.

"I would never ask him to let me go!" Gabriela exclaimed above the power of voice.

It was decided then and there that Gabriela Tishma truly wasn't up for any vacation or spending any amount of time away from her Erroneous Petroneus. Neither Alma nor Neli held that against her. It was just that Neli was surprised by the young Ms. Tishma's not comprehending the free lesson she had given them in how to handle a man as regards the questions for which a woman didn't actually need nor want an answer but simply a reaction. Neli Nizdlak almost managed to convince Alma Malarosa to have another talk with Gabriela Tishma but Alma didn't want to hear of it. She was an actress to be and for such a sensitive mind and spirit as was in possession of one Gabriela Tishma, to be dismayed from a decision already reached would take a thousand Homers and a thousand bards to override.

29

················ ✺ ················

oth Alma Malarosa and Neli Nizdlak managed to pack under twenty kilograms of clothing and other accessories for their flight to Sardinia, which was a feat in its own right. Oli Uzdlak drove them to Nikola Tesla airport accompanied by Mata Gradinar because he was the only one who owned a car, less the gals wanted to take the No.72 bus from Zelenjak to the airport. There there were long and lustful kisses exchanged at the airport Alitalia gate after which the ladies went through passport control and straight through the Duty free shop as if it didn't exist for they knew too what kind of luxury they were headed for on the wondrous Italian island. They boarded the plane tight on time and as soon as they were runway bound and much to the surprise of Oli Uzdlak, Mata Gradinar got out his *Levels of Learning* bulging in his back pack which he had brought with him, and wrote inside the book the name of the carrier and the number of the flight, just to be on the safe side. Then he spoke:

"Good, they're going to be fine."

"Excuse me?" Oli Uzdlak said.

"Their plane, it'll land safely in Sardinia."

"You're not going to start behaving weird like you did at the Academy, are you? Because there's only so much room for crazy in my car," Oli Uzdlak said with some humor.

"Don't worry about it. Did you see how they passed by the Duty free shop? We've got nothing to worry about," Mata Gradinar said putting away his book.

"How I envy your unmarried status, Mata."

"What do you mean?"

"I gave Neli one of my credit cards, that's what I mean."

"Oh, cheer up. I'm sure she'll buy something nice for you too," Mata said trying to console the man.

"I'm sure that you're right. I'll probably get one of those: "Been there, done that" coffee mugs."

"There you go! And you were worried. C'mon, I'll treat you to an espresso at the bar," Mata said.

"Thank you, you're a good friend."

"Did you know that this was the first time that I wrote something in the book and the name Unionia Bank didn't come up?" Mata Gradinar was thinking aloud more than anything else as they headed towards the airport bar.

"What on earth are you talking about?!" Oli Uzdlak said concerned.

"Nothing, it's just that I've written this difficult book and now I don't know what to do with it."

"Maybe you should take it to a publisher," Oli suggested.

"In the end I probably will, but let's stick to coffee for now."

As they sat down at the bar there could be heard the sounds of planes landing and taking off. One of those taking off was the carrier of Alma Malarosa and Neli Nizdlak now well-buckled into their seats, reaching their optimal takeoff speed on the bumpy runway of the only airport in Darol Jihad (which was how the Turks used to call Belgrade and it meant: "The city of wars"). As the Alitalia airplane set into a gradual climbing path so did the two ladies adjust their seats in an upright position of which they were cautioned to do by the onrushing stewardess who spoke perfect, fluent English.

"Excuse me dear, now that I've got you here, I need to know when will they begin serving the drinks," Neli Nizdlak asked the stewardess.

"Be patient, ma'am, the drinks will be served as soon we reach the cruising altitude of eight thousand kilometers."

The stewardess barely sauntered back to her post seeing how the plane was still in its steep and steady rise. She managed to get to her seat and buckle herself in.

"Oh, I have a text message from Mata!" Alma Malarosa said.

"Really, and what does it say?" Neli wanted to now.

"It reads: 'Don't worry, you'll have a safe flight, I consulted with the book.'"

"I wish my Oli would send me a message. I mean it's not like his thumbs have falled off," Neli said a bit jealous.

Their City of Wars was becoming ever smaller up until the point in which it looked like a model of an architect, fresh away from his drawing desk and T-square. All of the houses and blocks of the big city were now taken over by the sight of terracotta colored tiled roofs of the surrounding villages. In the distance they could see – as the plane made its twists and turns – the Bridge on the Ada, looking as majestic as a poet's lyre, but not quite there yet. It was at that point that the Alitalia plane made another and, as it turned out, final push for the heights towards which it aspired to, in other word to which it was mandated to climb and pretty soon there was nothing but clouds and the cool, soothing air debunking the theory of the heat of the sun – though it was very bright. There wasn't even a hint of turbulence as they flew over the Western Balkans and the overall weather seemed to do justice to their final destination when – right in the middle of the service, with all variety of drinks at hand – Neli Nizdlak got a message from her husband reading: "Don't drink too much on the plane, you know it makes you sick to your stomach. If you get a chance, ask Alma about Mata's book titled *Levels of Learning*."

*   *   *

When Mata got back from the bathroom Oli Uzdlak put his cell phone away post haste, but Mr. Gradinar couldn't help but pick through his mask of contentment with himself and realized that something had transpired while he had been away from their table. And if there was one thing that Mata hated the most it was people working on his behalf but behind his back. He, Mata, naturally surmised that it had something to do about the book and was now cursing himself for having brought it along to bid farewell to his Alma for whom he knew wouldn't pry into anything concerning any aspect of his work however devious that work might seem to others. But it was too late now. He knew, Oli Uzdlak knew about the book and there was nothing Mata Gradinar could do about that. But speaking of deviant behavior, one thought did cross his mind which was to put, or rather, write his, Oli's, name in the book and see what comes up. For now at least Mata decided to abstain from such devious actions provoked – admittedly so – by his own carelessness regarding him taking the book to no less a public place than an airport, which was, by the by, the first time that his original *Levels of Learning* had left his apartment. And again, as many a time before, the book made him act arrogant to the point of being insufferable; quite uncouth and roguish towards anyone in whose company he was reveling just a while ago, and this time that "a while" was in the presence of the husband of his girlfriend's best friend.

30

⸻ ∽ ⸻

The heat and the humidity – which must've been in the upper eighties – was well upon them once Oli Uzdlak and Mata Gradinar got onto the highway which led them back into the city. Along the way there lay scorched cornfields and a rare piece of land purchased by an investor for further development but left vacant for now. Above the crows were perched on high wires and nestled in the branches of the high poplar trees growing by the side of the highway. Luckily, Oli's car was air-conditioned, needless to say but worth the mention that without the cool air inside the vehicle Mata – who was otherwise prone to sweating – would have been dripping rapids through his shirt and the crotch of his pants.

Sooner than they had expected they passed the mark of entering the city when they drove by the West Belgrade Gate, an exquisite building which rose to the skies in the shape of two silos which were connected by a bridge at the top floor. The windows were round and the old West Gate served predominantly as a business space. Though once the pride of the city – which also had the East Gate on the opposite side – its grey concrete exterior represented only the waste and disrepair of the city's overall infrastructure. Having said that, the two friends were headed straight to the Gazela bridge which was reconstructed not so long ago for fear of it completely collapsing under the load of traffic it had to endure on a daily basis.

There was no conversation between the two men in the car as they got onto the Mostar Loop and onto the overpass for the simple reason that – although he had passed his driving exam and did have a license – Mata Gradinar didn't yet own a car. It was because of this that Oli extended an offer to him to drive him straight to his building, which Mata accepted as long as Oli would stay for a beer which was more than meeting Mata half-way as far as Mr. Uzdlak was concerned. As they left the rows of highway poplar trees behind, they got into Nemanjina Street where there grew, in two rows and lined one after another young sycamore trees that also provided a nice cool home for the crows. And as surely as Oli's car speed began to decrease this provided much room for conversation. They decided to keep it short and brief so the main topic of conversation was their two girls who were by now surely somewhere over Bosnia surely.

"It'll be good," Oli said.

"What's that?"

"This will be. To have some time apart from our better halves."

"I'm sure you're right, but I already miss my Alma."

"Oh, do quit it, Mata."

"I'm trying, but I can't. I love her too much."

"You really are smitten, aren't you?"

"Smitten? There's an understatement. Rope me, wheel me in and saddle me up, because I'm ready to go," Mr. Gradinar said.

"Boy, it's a good thing that your Alma didn't hear you say that."

"Now why is that?"

"Well, usually when women hear those types of confessions or professions of love they run for the mountains and don't look back," Mr. Uzdlak added.

"So this is the voice of matrimony talking, is it?"

"No, it's a voice of common sense accumulated over a lifetime which leads to matrimony," Oli said.

"Well, I can see your point, but surely you can't argue against the validity of what I'm feeling, can you?"

"I don't know what to say to you, friend. Time apart is time apart, but knowing you and Alma it'll only bring you closer together. Have the two of you ever travel as a couple?" Oli asked again.

"Yes, when I was a student we travelled Europe by rail, why do you ask?"

"You just answered your own question, buddy. Now, where's that house of yours?" Oli said as he was leaning over the steering wheel looking at street signs.

"Just make a turn here."

"A turn it is. Son of a…, you have a parking lot in your courtyard?!"

"Yea. Just let me get out and unlock the gates," Mata said as he got out the side door.

"Check first if there's any room for me to park!" Oli shouted through the window crack in his door.

"Of course there is, it's vacation season," Mr. Gradinar said.

As soon as Mata Gradinar closed the gate to his courtyard parking lot he foreboded an uneasy feeling in his stomach. This prompted him to hasten Mr. Uzdlak in his parking and once they were outside in the street and headed towards Mr. Gradinar's entrance his stomach started making growling noises.

"Don't worry. A beer would do us both good," Mr. Uzdlak said.

"It's not the beer I'm worried about."

And upon that utterance Mata Gradinar grabbed his stomach and squirmed, bending in his waist. Once he was in an upright position again he saw – as did Mr. Uzdlak – that the front door of his building was broken into in what was obviously a robbery. His recovery was as swift as was his gait as he ran into his house, backpack and all. He ran up the stairs and passed Mr. Yanisha Paroshki along the way on the second floor who cried after him:

"I'm so sorry, my boy. I simply didn't hear anything!" he exclaimed not aware of the loudness with which he did so.

Slowly but surely Mr. Uzdlak followed in the footsteps of Mr. Gradinar, granted not at such a speed but never the less with as much concern as was displayed by his host. He also passed Mr. Yanisha Paroshki on the second floor.

"Please, sir, let me come with you!" Mr. Paroshki begged of Mr. Uzdlak.

"By all means," Mr. Uzdlak said not fully understanding the request.

Having gotten there first, Mata Gradinar found that his apartment had been ransacked. The slip covers of his couch were cut open with what obviously was a knife. What was worse, he also found that whoever broke in managed to open the credenza. Lucky for him that he had brought the book with him to the airport for that was his primary suspicion: whoever was the culprit was searching for his *Levels of Learning*. He just wanted to check and establish one more fact before Mr. Uzdlak and Mr. Paroshki came up and into his apartment – the key, had they bothered to look for the key to the credenza in the bathroom medicine cabinet. Mr. Gradinar quickly established that no such attempt was made on the part of the burglars, so when Mr. Uzdlak and Mr. Paroshki did finally come into console him with words of comfort and pats on the back Mr. Gradinar realize that this was done by someone who firstly had wanted the book, and secondly had wanted to send a very strong message to Mata Gradinar.

The next order of business was to call the police which he did while at the same time asking both of his present companions to remain with him until the police finished their job. He also decided – but kept it to himself – to call Erroneous Petroneus, but this only after all was said and done as concerning the procedures of the treatment of the crime scene, if you could call it that for there was nothing missing from the apartment that wasn't there before. The only thing that was missing were the notes he had made while watching the morning program and news which he had wanted to put in his book.

31

························ ⌒〜⌒ ························

As soon as they came to the threshold of Mr. Gradinar's apartment, both Mr. Uzdlak and Mr. Paroshki's very reactions to the scene was brought to a halt. Unlike Mata neither of them knew what had transpired, so while Mr. Gradinar grabbed the receiver of his phone which was lying on the floor and dialed the police (192), his two companions entered the apartment and began surveying it as if they were in awe of the chaos which the perpetrator or perhaps perpetrators had committed. Aside from that there wasn't really anything to add besides Mr. Paroshki's futile attempts of professing his innocence to Mata Gradinar. He did so by stating – even before the police had arrived – that he had heard nothing seeing how he had been in the middle of one of his guitar lessons. That coupled by the fact Mr. Paroshki was half-deaf in one ear made Mata Gradinar give him a pardon therefore relieving the aging man in what was surely a sincere act of penitence. Concerning Mr. Uzdlak, he was more curious than anything else. He wanted to know – and expressed it directly – who did Mata Gradinar think the perpetrators or perpetrator were.

"How am I supposed to know?" was the answer Mata gave.

"I'm not sure entirely but I think it's all due to that book of yours that I've seen you logging around with."

"Don't be absurd! I carry many things with me in my backpack. So what of it if my book is one of them?"

Under a barrage of such questions Mata Gradinar thought that he was already talking to the police. And then, suddenly a patrol car pulled over by the curb of his building and two officers came out of the police vehicle. It being that the front door was already broken, they made their way up to the third floor where Mata Gradinar was in a long awaiting state, pacing all over the place as if trying to conjure up some explanation to the officers on his point of view as to who might have committed the break in.

"Here they come, Mata," Mr. Yanisha Paroshki said with a solemn tone in his voice.

Upon stepping on the stairwell landing of the third floor, one of the two officers asked who was the person who made the call.

"I called you officer. Please, come in," Mata said politely.

"I'm officer Gospodar Džigerousni and this is my partner officer Poslugar Dadaković.

"Now, let's have a look, shall we," Džigerousni, who was obviously in charge, said.

"First you must know something, sir," Mr. Paroshki said.

"And what's that?" Džigerousni asked.

"I'm only the downstairs neighbor and I didn't hear anything. You see, I was giving a guitar lesson, that's it…"

"There'll be enough time for talking later at the police station for you, mister…?"

"Paroshki. Yanisha Paroshki," he said.

"Mister Gradinar, have I got that right?" Džigerousni asked Mata. "Is this your apartment?"

"Yes. This is my apartment."

"Is there something missing? Have they taken something?"

"No, there's nothing missing," Mata said.

"It seems to me to be nothing more than an act of vandalism," Mr. Uzdlak felt compelled to add.

"Does it now?" said Džigerousni.

All the while his partner officer Dadaković remained as silent as a mermaid spotting a ship on the horizon. But there was no question about it, and after a short explanation the two policemen explained to them why all three of them had to go to the precinct. And so they moved slowly down the three flights of stairs, stopping at the second floor to provide Mr. Paroshki with the opportunity to change from his pajamas into some decent clothes. After waiting for him to pick out the perfect outfit for a police precinct they re-embarked on their descent down the stairs. Officer Džigerousni lead the way while officer Dadaković was in the back, right behind Mata Gradinar and his bulging backpack which this one held in his left hand so as not to arouse any possible curious questions on the part of the police as to the content of the backpack.

They were headed to the city's primary police stations in Despot Stefan's Boulevard No.107. As for the three unfortunate souls seated in the back, they could only watch in dismay at the condition of the building, never mind the fact that atop its roof it housed a helicopter landing pad, in fact one helicopter was just about to land as they were escorted into the station. Mata Gradinar though that this was no usual surrounding. He had an eerie suspicion that the three of them were brought here for reasons quite different than those he had originally anticipated while he was making the 192 call.

"Have a seat on this bench, gentlemen, yes, right across from that room. You'll be called in when your time comes," Gospodar Džigerousni explained.

"Don't worry; I'll keep my eye on them," Poslugar Dadaković said to his partner.

It felt as if they'd been waiting for hours as other civilians went in and out of the room which at first seemed to them to be ready solely for the three of them. Yanisha Paroshki was still vehemently stating his case to the still standing by their side officer Dadaković and being completely ignored by the seasoned yet young looking policeman. Meanwhile Oli Uzdlak couldn't help but notice that – seated right next to him – Mata Gradinar was clutching his backpack so tightly that the outlines of the book could be seen under the fabric from which it was made.

"You had to bring that cursed thing, didn't you?" Oli asked in light of the book.

"Never you mid what I carry with me," was Mata's reply.

"I damn will mind if it lands me in a police station!" Oli spoke above the power of voice.

"Keep it quiet, you two, you're disturbing the inspector!" officer Dadaković said.

And for one brief moment there was utter silence on the bench in front of the inspector's office while through the glass portion of the door there was seen a silhouette of a man who then opened the door ajar and a bald head protruded through the narrow space.

"Officer, which one of them is the victim?" the inspector said.

"The one in the middle, sir, a Mister Gradinar."

"Well, Mister Gradinar, won't you come in. I assure you it won't take but a minute."

Mata Gradinar stood up and the inspector opened his door as wide as it could open. In any case, Mata was offered a chair at the inspector's desk so he sat down while the door was shut with the loud noise of the glass and wood chiming in unison. The first thing which the inspector noticed about Mata's person was his back pack and he therefore asked him:

"You don't part lightly with your possessions, do you, Mister Gradinar?"

"It depends. Why do you ask?"

"You could've left your backpack on the bench. I said that this would only take a minute."

"My work is in here; my graduate paper."

"And you're a student of…?"

"Pedagogy. But I no longer study it; I work in that field at present."

"Oh, my dear boy, to work is to study… May I take a look at it?"

"I'd rather you didn't."

It was then that the inspector's demeanor and the prior mild and almost soothing lines of his countenance were turned into something ominous and foreboding. He said that all three of them were free to leave at their own will but not without uttering to Mr. Gradinar the strangest phrase this one could've expected from a police inspector:

"The truth is irrelevant as long as one is in possession of information."

32

The next day Mata Gradinar woke up in a thunderous morning. As he was making his Eggs Benedict breakfast he seriously considered skipping work altogether, but seeing how he had already taken a day's leave of absence he had no choice but to head to Queen Natalia Street No.43 and at least try to give some sense to his future existence as a professional in pedagogy. He also made the decision to bring along his original *Levels of Learning* to show to Professor Neven Goryan. He had made such a decision not out of want to brag about what he had stumbled into, but as an – let's call it – alibi for any and all future woes that he might encounter such as last night's break in.

Mata Gradinar showered and shaved and was hoping not to run into any of the neighbors, especially into Mr. Yanisha Paroshki. But he had no such luck. Things being how they were – and this included Mr. Paroshki's habit of going out to buy the paper at 6.00 in the morning – the two met on the ground floor where the repair men were working on fixing the front door of the building which had been broken into yesterday.

"Won't you join me for a cup of coffee?" Mr. Paroshki asked Mata.

"Thank you, sir, but I must go to work. Perhaps some other time?"

"Don't think you'll get out of it; I have the memory of an elephant. And there you go again with that backpack of yours."

"I really am sorry, Mister Paroshki, but I don't have the time. Besides don't you have students to teach today?"

"You know you're right. I completely forgot about my guitar lessons. You know, Mister Gradinar, there's just one pupil of mine whom I'd really like you to hear play guitar. The child is a prodigy on the instrument."

"Yes, you mentioned this. I tell you what; when my girlfriend comes back from her trip to Sardinia we can organize a recital, you know, make an evening of it."

"A grand idea indeed. Let's do just that, it's high time the boy played in front of strangers. Well, I won't keep you any longer, Mister Gradinar, so goodbye for now."

"Goodbye, Mister Paroshki."

Mata passed through a narrow space which was once the front door but was now occupied by the workmen. It was raining outside and the humidity was unbearable. He took out his umbrella and it seemed to him that the whole city did fit under it. For reasons unknown, weather-wise of course, he decided to walk to work for which he indeed did have the time, but considering the downpour was a very bad and ill-considered idea. Still he braved through it all with the cats hiding under parked cars and stray dogs as if in a trot running right next to the walls of the buildings, and of course the pedestrians – few of whom were caught in the rain with no umbrella for it had been pouring since first light – rushing to work.

He rushed into the Faculty of Pedagogy building just about the time that the rain began to turn into hail. Once inside he folded his umbrella back into a more practical shape (practical for carrying) and headed straight to professor Goryan's office. With a knock on the door and a single shout of "come in!" he met his first boss ever. It goes without saying that the professor reprimanded him for missing his first day at work, but he did it almost in jest and the good humor for which he was known throughout the faculty. Professor Goryan offered Mata a cup of coffee which this one didn't refuse and began briefing him on the jobs that he'd be assisting him with for that day and – as he put it, also in good humor – perhaps for many days to come.

What struck Mata Gradinar at the outset was that professor Goryan was one of the few people that he knew or rather the only person whom he knew who didn't ask a single question about his backpack and the contents thereof. It was precisely for this reason that Mata decided to show and share his original graduate paper with the professor. But just as he was about to unzip his backpack and get out the bulging book which has grown in volume quite a bit since he first picked it up at the Fahmor bookbinders, professor Neven Goryan said he had to attend an urgent staff meeting before the lecturing begins, leaving Mata Gradinar alone with his unfulfilled intention and a cup of good, warm coffee.

Mr. Gradinar was pretty happy with himself. He had a desk of his own which already contained a to-do pile on it, being how he missed a day of work. The to-do pile consisted primarily of administrative papers which the students used to postpone the time of their exams and such. He didn't want to mess things up on his first day in the professor's office so he left the work waiting until professor Neven Goryan returned from the staff meeting. On the other hand, Mata was incredibly curious as to the content of the professor's desk which looked like a chaotic experiment in administrative paperwork and how to make it even more unbearable.

Professor Goryan was never known for his tidiness but on the other hand he was the pinnacle of punctuality and multitasking for what seemed as little bits of shards of paper laying on a desk to Mata Gradinar and anyone else who might stumble into the office was in fact the precise order in which the professor liked his business to be organized without ever getting confused. In other words, he didn't care whether a butterfly flaps his wings or not, he just cared whether he knew the species or not and from there on end he could derive the rest with which he was previously unclear about.

It seemed that only a few minutes had gone by when the professor returned; it seemed so, but only to Mata Gradinar who spent the time of his absence from the office going over his own pile of administrative to do work. And when he caught him not even noticing his entrance, the professor just patted Mata on the back and said:

"You and I are going to get along just fine."

"Believe me, sir, after looking at your desk, and please pardon the indiscretion, I was of the mind to give up, but decided to let it alone. We will be working on separate matters, right?"

"Of course we are. And thank you for not moving any of my stuff around, or try to make some sense of order out of it because this is how my perfect universe looks like," the professor said proudly while pointing towards his desk.

"One more thing, sir, your lecture is due in five minutes," Mata said.

"So I've got plenty of time."

"Not according from what I found on my desk. You have a lot of postponed exams to preside over, and I don't think your busy schedule will allow you a moment to spare."

"Show me."

Professor Goryan briskly stood up and walked over to Mata's desk. He couldn't believe his eyes as to the amount of work that had piled up since Mr. Gradinar's generation had graduated. In a very much apologetic manner, the professor asked Mr. Gradinar to stay after his lectures so that they might come up with some kind of system of dealing with these slackers because – let's face it – most students had postponed taking their exams because they hadn't studied enough, or because they thought they had something better to do. Most youth gets caught up in such moments of weakness, which is why youth is always forgiven.

33

················ ⌀ ················

Perilously close to losing track of time while still at work, Mata Gradinar received high praise from professor Goryan by marking all the relevant and urgent student cases in one segment which were to be examined by the professor right away and the irrelevant one's in the segment he marked as insufficient. He managed to get so much work done while the professor was lecturing all thanks' to his book into which he would write down every and any single student's name of whom he wanted to learned more than what the said student had written on a piece of paper in citing his or her excuse – in other words he was able to find out the truth.

What Mata Gradinar didn't know however was that the police inspector had put officers Džigerousni and Dadaković in charge of surveilling him wherever he may go, especially if he, and when he, was carrying his backpack with him. The case being such, officer Džigerousni waited for Mata to come out of Queen Natalia No.43, while officer Dadaković waited across the way, in front of the Obstetrics Hospital. The two policemen, now dressed in civilian clothing, were to communicate via cell phone so as not to arouse suspicion. Finally after a good half an hour's wait in front of the Pedagogical Faculty building, officer Džigerousni cued officer Dadaković by pointing at Mata Gradinar who was walking down the steps and onto the sidewalk where he turned, heading straight towards Beograđanka all waiting for him in his black sail and he the son of Ilium. The undercover officers had no idea where the young man they were following was headed but they had their orders. It was obvious that out of the two of them Džigerousni was the one in charge while Dadaković was simply answering every instruction by repeating into his cell phone the words "yes, yes". But to give the officers some credit they did cover their mark pretty well. Mata Gradinar had no idea he was being followed though he did perceive a notion of someone playing the part of his shadow as he entered deeper and deeper into his neighborhood, where the streets became smaller and quieter.

Eventually Mata turned onto Kumanovska Street and headed a few paces downwards towards the Boulevard. With a single "yes" Dadaković found himself crossing Krunska Street and by the side of Džigerousni who pointed to the sign of the store into which Mr. Gradinar had gone into.

-"Fahmor Bookbinders (est. 1923)" Džigerousni spoke and had Dadaković put it down into his notes.

"I'll alert the inspector, shall I?" Dadaković asked.

"Yes, but keep in mind that we don't have anything concrete as yet."

"Yes, of course."

Therefore Dadaković dialed the office number of the inspector and brought him up to speed on their progress as concerned Mata Gradinar. The conversation didn't last for long and mostly consisted of Dadaković repeating his well-practiced "yes, yes".

"Well, what did the inspector say?" Džigerousni asked his partner.

"He said that we were to wait until Mister Gradinar comes out of the store and then go in ourselves to question the book-binder, if at all we find him." Dadaković said.

"Did the inspector mention whether we should introduce ourselves as the police or not when we go into the store?"

"Yes."

"Yes what?"

"Yes, we should show our badges," officer Dadaković said.

But all the while and what the policeman didn't know was that the store in Kumanovska Street had a back exit, which is far from the point and purpose as to why Mata Gradinar went inside in the first place.

It was because he had decided that he wanted desperately to get rid of the book. Yes, he did find the owner, Mister Bleh Fahmor there but Mister Fahmor wouldn't hear of it for his reasoning was that as long as the book already had a title there was nothing he could do about it. And no matter how much Mata Gradinar pleaded with him and tried to explain his situation by even mentioning the break-in at his apartment, Mr. Bleh Fahmor wouldn't hear of it.

"Just be careful what you write in your *Levels of Learning*," Mr. Fahmor advised.

"But that's just the thing, sir, that's not my title for it. I didn't even have a clue until my friend though it up," Mr. Gradinar was trying to get away with something and Mr. Fahmor sensed it.

"No, Mister Gradinar, I'm afraid that the business between us is concluded. I understand that at first that didn't appear to be the case, but the fact is that it has been concluded for a long while; you're just beginning to realize it now."

"I'm sorry for being so pushy, sir."

"Given your predicament, it's understandable," Mr. Fahmor said.

As soon as Mata turned around towards the exit he immediately spotted officers Džigerousni and Dadaković hanging round the corner across the way in a most conspicuous manner. He hastily turned to Bleh Fahmor with a final plead:

"Sir, does this store have a back door?"

"Why, yes it does. Why?"

"I have no time to explain. I think that those two gentlemen will explain it better than me if they were here," Mata pointed at the two men besides the front door of the bookbinders.

"Don't worry. Come with me," Mr. Fahmor said.

"Thank you, sir. I don't know how to repay you," Mr. Gradinar said as they were about to part ways.

"Just promise me that you won't be bothering me with that book of yours anymore."

"Done, sir! You have my word."

And so Mata Gradinar vanished behind the back exit of the bookbinders. The reason why such a type of store would have a back door was quite simple: it was meant for getting all the necessary work material inside without causing congestion in the traffic of Kumanovska Street.

It took them a while but after some time officers Džigerousni and Dadaković decided to go into the bookbinders themselves to check on what was going on. After all, they had to report something to the inspector. But just about the time they were crossing the street the two officers spotted a young man's hand turn over the card which was hanging in the front door and both Gospodar Džigerousni and Poslugar Dadaković saw it in fine Serbian language print: ON BREAK. They both knew that if they don't report this turn of events to the inspector there'd be hell to pay, so naturally it was mutually decided that officer Dadaković should make the call which he did.

Surprisingly enough the inspector didn't react quite the way that the two officers had expected. As it turned out, the inspector was just curious about the content of Mr. Gradinar's backpack because – being an informed man and having sources of his own – he found it funny; the whole break-in business into the apartment of someone who has just graduated from University. Additionally, the inspector also knew very well, or at least he had heard of Mister Gradinar's rise to prominence in the academic circles for he was told of this young talented man whom the students from other Faculties that had come to listen to him when he was defending his graduate paper, the title of which the inspector couldn't get out of his head: *Levels of Learning*.

34

⚓

rroneous and Gabriela were lying on top of each other, moving like a stormy sea, when the phone rang all rude and uncouth interrupting their sweaty like state of loveforging. It was Mata on the other line saying to Erroneous that he had to come over right away. After a minutes protest in which – while covering the speaker of the receiver with his hand – Erroneous had a brief disagreement with Gabriela about whether they should let him come over or not due to the fact they weren't finished, Tish said:

"So let's finish now, together."

"Simultaneously?" Petroneus asked perplexed.

"Of course, silly."

"Come over in about twenty minutes, Mata. Gabriela has to get ready for work," Erroneous spoke into the receiver and then hung up the phone all the while still managing to keep his erection.

"U-u-u, Gabriela has to get ready for work!" she said as she tickled his belly.

"Was I lying?" Erroneous asked.

"Holly loafs, we really need to wrap things up here," Tish said having taken a look at his night stand clock.

It was nothing more than a simple missionary position but Erroneous worked it with such speed that she almost popped the top of her head off. He put a pillow under her waist so that she too could manipulate her hips. Gabriela was whispering his name while calling out to God as if in a carnal prayer for the thing that he was doing to her to never stop. But as bad fortune would have it, at one point she did turn her head towards the night stand with the clock and began spurring him on moaning, "Now, baby, now!" What did he know but to obey his Tish, and for the record she didn't fake it for her nipples were as pink as rose blossoms in high spring and her skin was a taste of an amalgam of salty and sweet.

She said she didn't want any breakfast but that she just wanted to use the shower before Mata came along. Erroneous got her a fresh, clean towel and hence until he had finished with his breakfast she disappeared in the bathroom. Some minutes later Gabriela Tishma came out of the shower with her hair all dry and she was all dressed and ready to go to the bakery. Luckily for Erroneous she wasn't a baker or occurrences like this wouldn't be possible; but she was rather only a sales girl, giving people what they would order, charge them and work the till.

After Gabriela left him with a kiss and departed from their apartment with a scent of wild cherry blossoms on her skin, dressed all in white, Erroneous Petroneus could hear the chit chat between her and Mata on the stair landing, right in front of the elevator. The two were discussing the fact that Erroneous and Gabriela had never taken a trip together and – and this came from Mata's mouth – seeing how Mr. Petroneus had vacation time coming it would be refreshing for them to go and travel somewhere together. But to the question:

"Then how come you are not in Sardinia with Alma if you think this way?"

Mr. Gradinar just grinned and tried to explain that his situation was different, that he was just starting at his new job, and as the law mandates it, a citizen can't acquire vacation time in their first year of employment.

The last thing that Erroneous heard from the outer side of his front door was Gabriela saying to Mata:

"Nice backpack. It makes you look like your job. Ha, ha!"

"How very true, Gabriela. Is our banker decent in there or should I wait a while."

"Decent, ha! He's way above average. And no, you don't have to wait. Bye," she said from inside the elevator.

"Bye, Gabriela," Mata responded.

As soon as he heard that Mata Gradinar brought that backpack with him Erroneous Petroneus knew that he had also brought the book. He was honestly beginning to feel as if his friend was taking advantage of his good nature and mild temper. Erroneous had specifically requested that Mata show him nothing from that book; he didn't want to know anything about it for ever since the book came into use strange things began happening, least of which was his encounter with the old Gypsy woman on the corner of Molerova and Krunska Streets. But as it turned out, Mata Gradinar didn't mention the book other than to say that his apartment was broken into and that he was introduced to two new characters in his life, namely – and he did name them – officers Džigerousni and Dadaković.

"Then what brings you here if not the famous book?" Erroneous asked.

"I need a loan."

"A loan for what?"

"It appears that Neli Nizdlak and my Alma lost their wallets on the beach in Sardinia," Mata said.

"So shouldn't this be a concern for one Oli Uzdlak? He is Neli's husband, isn't he?"

"Yes, and I completely agree with you. But I'm just on my way to the bank now and I have no money to transfer to Alma. And as concerns Missus Nizdlak, well, she's too proud to call her husband for help."

"Oh how I love it when a banker is needed. You people think that you've got it all figured out as to how to do things better, but at the first sign of the ship sinking and to whom do you turn: to the banker."

"Please don't make me beg this favor of you, I miss my Malarosa enough as it is. And if this happened solely by chance then at least let me provoke a favorable reaction from my love in helping her by means of which I'll speak nothing but good from now on."

"I don't care who you mention. I just want you to promise one single thing in return," Erroneous said.

"Name it and it shall be done."

"I want you to promise that I will never have anything to do with *that* book again."

"What?"

"You heard me. I want no part in your Levels of Learning from now on. Will you abide by such an agreement?"

"Yes. Sadly so, but yes," Mata Gradinar said with a bow of his head.

"A-ha! Don't worry; this is not mockery on my part. I too much like that the other mortals feel good when I'm wanted. So, how much money are we talking about?"

"A thousand euros or so."

"Don't give me that "or so". Let me have an exact amount," Erroneous insisted.

"A thousand and five hundred, okay?"

"That's more like it. But why on earth would they choose Sardinia of all places to take their vacation. Didn't they know that it's a prime location for the rich and famous? How were they going to cover all of those costs of going out, and shopping, don't get me started on the shopping. I assume you have your Alma's bank account number?"

"Yes, she texted it to me. You know, they arrive tomorrow. And as far as expenses go, you'd be surprised how much a tooth paste commercial can bring in, I certainly was," Mata said.

"I wouldn't know anything about that. But I guarantee you they'll be back both of them with a new suitcase each."

Erroneous Petroneus then told Mata Gradinar to wait in the living room while he took a shower with the bathroom all smelling of Gabriela Tishma; so much of her was left behind in those aromas that the poor Erroneous almost got a new erection which he averted by taking an icy cold shower. When he was finished he got dressed and in his suit and tie while sporting a fine leather brief case he escorted Mata Gradinar to the lobby where they parted ways, but this was only after they got outside; each his own way and each on his own task be it the Pedagogical Faculty or the Unionia Bank.

35

.... ❧ ....

They were the working hours that Mata Gradinar was spending – much to the extent of his patience – in professor Goryan's office. And having been so highly praised by his superior, he found that the other professors wanted to make use of him as well, so whenever he was on break Mata would sneak out to the staff cafeteria carrying his book and hide away until this particular work day was done at which point – or so he expected – Oli Uzdlak was to come and pick him up to go to the airport for it was the day of their lovers' return from Sardinia. The staff cafeteria had a TV screen, and having remembered those notes of his which were stolen in the break in and not having seen the news that morning, but most of all out of arrogance coupled with curiosity; he opened the book and wrote with a steady hand:

"THE MINISTRY OF THE INTERIOR".

First the name of the Minister appeared, a certain Slava Pendrek after which all of his corrupt political history came into

Mata's view along with Mr. Pendrek's private affairs such as the now infamous but forgotten under-the-sands of the aforementioned gentleman's rehabilitation in the political sphere: "The Suitcase Affair". Suddenly, as the book was getting filled by all the need-to-know information – and Mata Gradinar needed to know for he was the book's master – there was a flood of breaking news on the staff cafeteria TV set all of which involved Slava Pendrek under the heading:

"The Man and the Carrier We Forgot."

Having had his coffee and his fill of fun, not to mention his successful avoidance of the other professors who needed his favors, Mata Gradinar returned to Neven Goryan's office where he encountered a frightening scene. The thing of the matter and to the point of fact, he did find professor Goryan in the office, but much to his dismay there was also present officer Dadaković-the police equivalent of a yes man. Mr. Gradinar could tell as soon as he came in that the two were in some kind of deep and serious discussion, unfortunately he heard no names being mentioned. Another piece of that moments delight was Mata knocking on the door which was left open all with his book under his arm to wit he could spy a grin on officer Dadaković's face. The professor, on the other hand, thought nothing of it and informed officer Dadaković that the book his assistant was carrying was his famous graduate paper entitled *Levels of Learning*. Still and regardless of the familial atmosphere into which officer Poslugar Dadaković had stumbled, he insisted that Mata Gradinar come in with a 'Hi'. And that was the problem for Mr. Gradinar never found it necessary to explain his book to the good professor who obviously said to the impatient officer that Mata was free for the day and that officer Dadaković could certainly take him away.

"Don't worry, my boy. The officer explained it all to me. I'm so sorry that your apartment was broken into."

Mata Gradinar knew he had no way of getting out of this. He couldn't mention his girlfriend, firstly because he didn't want her to suffer along with what he had perceived was his fate and a *fait accompli* at that. And secondly, even if he were to mention Alma Malarosa and the airport pickup he knew he would also have to mention Oli Uzdlak who was his ride to the airport and he was wise to the fact that officer Dadaković knew who Oli was for he and officer Džigerousni had already brought both of them, including the unwitting neighbor Mr. Paroshki, to the police station.

"You'll hear from me yet," Mata Gradinar said to the professor above the power of voice as he was led out of the office by officer Dadaković who reminded him to pack his book into the backpack which lay resting by the leg of his table.

He was led outside in the company of the officer and to a sight he had dreaded but expected: a parked police car with the inspector in the back seat and officer Džigerousni at the wheel.

"In the back," said officer Dadaković.

"Where are we going?" Mata asked.

He received no answer to his pertinent query, at least it seemed pertinent to him while, on the other hand, the atmosphere in the car was more than relaxed when they pulled away from the curb and joined the rest of the motorized traffic at the inspectors command.

Once they had reached Nemanjina Street they turned at the traffic light. It was then that Mata Gradinar realized that they were headed towards New Belgrade.

"You youths are something else. That's what I think, Mister Gradinar, don't you agree?" the inspector spoke.

"I don't understand my transgression. What law have I broken?" Mata said.

"The basic laws of the new society."

"Please explain, inspector."

"You see, my young friend, there are no more ideologies. What were once ideologies are today simply technical tools we use to, let us say, mend the wounds of our new brave society. But obviously, you didn't understand that, so you may think of this meeting of ours as the last one."

"Of course there are ideologies…" Mata tried to get a word in.

"No, no there are none. And you have proof of it right there in your little backpack, and you know very well the reason why you've kept it a secret so far."

"Why is that?"

"So that no innocent man shall die."

*   *   *

It was at that point that a car pulled up to the building of the Pedagogical Faculty, and Oli Uzdlak went in and straight to the professor's office after asking around as to its location architecturally wise.

"You must be professor Neven Goryan," Oli said upon shaking hands with the man.

"Yes. And you must be Oli Uzdlak; Mata speaks very highly of you."

"Is he here? I'm supposed to take him to the airport."

"Oh, no. He's long gone, Mata was taken by the police. An officer Dadaković, if I recall."

"The Police?! I apologize, professor, but I really must go."

"But how will you find him?"

Oli answered with a wave of his hand as he was exiting the office and then it dawned on him that something bad was about to happen to Mata Gradinar. Having no other choice he got in his car and, ironically, took the same route as the police car which took Mata away.

*   *   *

"Here is fine. No one will see us here. Stop the car, officer," the inspector ordered.

As Mata Gradinar looked up he saw the high-rise of the West Belgrade gate along with its bridge mounted at the top of the cylindrical structure.

"Hand cuff him, will you, officer Dadaković?" the inspector ordered.

"Yes, sir."

The two policemen in full uniform led Mata Gradinar by his elbows with his hands handcuffed behind his back with the inspector following them carrying Mata's backpack with him.

*   *   *

Along his route, Oli Uzdlak passed the Western Belgrade Gate, driving on the highway on his way to the airport. In a text message he informed Neli Nizdlak that Mata Gradinar wouldn't be able to make it, that he was still at work. Naturally he was lying to spare Ms. Malarosa's feelings.

*   *   *

The small group headed up by the inspector took the elevator all the way to the top floor. They held on to Mata while the inspector was following them as close as a shadow can follow one's foot. When they came to the half-way point of the bridge the inspector ordered the two officers to get the man in custody down on his knees while he emptied the contents of Mr. Gradinar's backpack onto the hard floor right by Mata's side. He made a few joking comments about the view from the tallest point of the building and then he ordered officer Poslugar Dadaković to execute the offender of the new society, as the inspector had put it. The officer ram his knee into the back of Mata Gradinar's knee sending this one straight to the ground at which point Mata heard the inspector mumble into his chin the words:

"You could've made a nice life for yourself here. Just look at that view."

And Mr. Gradinar did abide the inspector's suggestion while a single tear rolled down one of his cheeks. The bridge of the Gate echoed throughout its surroundings with a single pistol shot and Mata Gradinar fell face down onto the floor in a kind of spasmodic motion.

He didn't die of his own will; he didn't die by his own hand.

FIN

SYNOPSIS

In the vein of Goethe's *Der Zauberlehrling*, Vignjevic's *Catalogue Diabolique* is a fantastical tale of Mata Gradinar, a newly appointed Pedagogical Faculty post-doc whose well-received graduate paper throws him into a world of secrets revealed by his work.

This all starts when he goes to the bookbinders to pick up his finished work where instead he finds that – although the book has been bound – there is no text on the pages. At first confused to the point of not even protesting, Mata Gradinar discovers that he has more than empty pages in his hands, but rather a catalog of empty pages that allows him to discover all the wrongdoers in his society. Mata then embarks to uncover all with the help of his best friend Eroneous Petroneus.

At first Mata Gradinar is extremely careful what he writes in the book, since everything he writes within it reveals the deep history, and possible future of that subject. As the tale develops so does Mata's curiosity with regard to his wanting to rid his society of all evil doing, primarily by exposing the vast corruption that surrounds him.

The story in the book has been carefully chosen by the author to emphasize the length to which corruption can spread in any given society, thereby diminishing the value that the same society puts on human life.

*   *   *

AUTHOR BIOGRAPHY

***

Mr. Vignjevic was born on the 9th of August, 1978 in Belgrade, Serbia. He first began writing poetry while in high school in 1994 only to graduate to fiction in 2005.

From 1987 to 1990 he lived with his family in Moscow, USSR where he attended a Russian grammar school along with both a Yugoslavian and music schools.

After finishing school in Belgrade, Mr. Vignjevic studied Law at Belgrade University only to drop out after one year. He then enrolled at the Faculty for International Management, European University from which he graduated in 2003. Since then he has been an active author, having published The Peacock Agenda in 2018, the play adaptation of which is to be forthcoming in 2020.

www.ingramcontent.com/pod-product-compliance
Lightning Source LLC
Chambersburg PA
CBHW021221260626
47172CB00002B/538